THE MOST INSPIRING SPORTS STORIES OF ALL TIME FOR KIDS!

THE ULTIMATE SPORT BOOK FOR KIDS AGES 8-12

MICHAEL LANGDON

CONTENTS

MIRACULOUS TEAMS

PERFECT 10 PERFORMANCES

BASKETBALL BEASTS

VOLLEYBALL VIRTUOSOS

GOLF GREATS

SOCCER SULTANS

AMERICAN FOOTBALL GREATS

TENNIS TITANS

BASEBALL BEHEMOTHS

DRIVING LEGENDS

HOCKEY HEROES

THE MENTALITY OF AN ATHLETE

FULL TIME!

TRIVIA TIME!

INTRODUCTION

"Sport has the power to change the world. It has the power to inspire. It has the power to unite people in a way that little else does. It speaks to youth in a language they understand. Sport can create hope where once there was only despair."

Nelson Mandela

———

Welcome, young readers, to an adventure like no other! In this book, "The Most Inspiring Sports Stories of All Time for Kids!", we'll dive into the amazing world of sports, where heroes are made, dreams come true, and every game is a chance to shine. Sports aren't just about winning or losing; they're about passion, determination, and the incredible power of teamwork.

Nelson Mandela's powerful words remind us that sports can do more than just entertain us—they can bring people together, lift our spirits, and help us believe in ourselves.

In the pages ahead, you'll read about brave athletes who overcame huge obstacles, legendary teams that worked together to achieve the impossible, and unforgettable moments that have inspired millions around the globe. From the soccer fields of Argentina to the powerful waves of the Pacific, from the basketball courts of the NBA to the running tracks of the Olympics, you'll discover stories that show how sports can be a force for good.

You'll meet heroes like Jim Abbott, who broke barriers in baseball and showed the world the power of courage and determination. You'll be inspired by the story of Wilma Rudolph, who overcame polio to become one of the fastest women in the world. And you'll cheer for the amazing teamwork of the 1980 U.S. Olympic hockey team, who proved that anything is possible with heart and hard work.

But this book isn't just about famous athletes and big events. It's also about the lessons we can learn from sports. At the end of each chapter, we'll see what lessons we can learn from the world's greatest athletes. You'll see how important it is to never give up, to always believe in yourself, and to be a good teammate. Whether you love playing sports or just enjoy watching them, these stories will inspire you to be the best you can be, both on and off the field.

So, get ready to be amazed, inspired, and motivated by the incredible tales of sportsmanship, perseverance, and triumph. Whether you're dreaming of scoring the winning goal, running the fastest race, or simply being the best version of yourself, remember: the power to achieve greatness is within you.

Let the games begin!

LEGENDS OF THE TRACK

CHAPTER 1
JESSE OWENS

RACING AGAINST UNFAIRNESS

THE 1930S WERE A TURBULENT TIME, BOTH IN THE UNITED STATES AND ACROSS THE ATLANTIC in Germany.

In America, racial segregation was a harsh reality, with African Americans facing inequalities and widespread discrimination. Meanwhile, Germany was under the rule of Adolf Hitler's Nazi regime, which promoted white people being better than everyone else.

It was against this backdrop of intense racial tension that Jesse Owens, an African American athlete, arrived at the 1936 Berlin Olympics, to mark one of the most significant events in sports history.

Owens' achievements at these games were monumental. He won four gold medals. One in the 100-meter race, one in the 200-meter race, one in the long jump competition, and one in the 4 × 100-meter relay.

By winning four gold medals, he not only challenged the notion of white supremacy but also showcased the heights that could be achieved through talent and determination, irrespective of race. His victories were a direct humiliation of the Nazi propaganda of racial superiority and resonated globally, providing a counter-narrative that championed equality and human dignity.

Imagine being in Owens' shoes, stepping onto the Olympic track in Berlin, surrounded by racist logos, and an audience screaming racist slurs at you. The pressure was immense. Not only was he representing his country in a highly politicized arena, but he also carried the hopes of millions of African Americans, yearning for a hero who could shatter the negative stereotypes that were incorrectly said about them.

During his preparation for the Olympics, Owens had limited access to training facilities because of the color of his skin, racial slurs from teammates, and even exclusion from certain competitions. Yet, at the Berlin Olympics, his interactions with other athletes, such as the German long-jumper Luz Long who offered Owens advice during competitions, highlighted moments of solidarity that overcame racial divides. This highlighted the undeniable unifying power of sports.

The ripple effects of Owens' success extended far beyond the confines of the Berlin Olympic Stadium. His triumphs challenged the prevailing racial ideologies of the time and provided hope for a better tomorrow. Athletes of all backgrounds were inspired by his courage, leading to greater participation and slowly changing perceptions in sports and beyond.

Despite his success on the track, Owens' battle did not end at the Berlin Olympics. Returning to America, he struggled with the realities of the racial prejudice that still lived in American society. Unlike many Olympic heroes, lucrative endorsements did not come his way, and he found himself racing against horses for entertainment to earn a living.

However, Owens' legacy prompted important conversations about race and sportsmanship. His legacy continues to pave the way for future generations of athletes to be treated equally, and his accomplishments that summer in 1936 remains the ultimate testament to the impact an athlete can have on the world, challenging societal norms and promoting a message of equality and resilience.

Scan the QR code to watch a video of Jesse Owens in action!

CHAPTER 2

WILMA RUDOLPH

THE TRIUMPH OF THE TENNESSEE SWIFT

WILMA RUDOLPH'S STORY BEGINS IN A CRAMPED HOUSE IN CLARKSVILLE, TENNESSEE, WHERE she was born the 20th of 22 siblings. Her early years were marked by a series of challenges that would have stopped many in their tracks.

Before Wilma was five, she faced lots of illnesses that made her very sick. These included double pneumonia, scarlet fever, and then polio—a disease that left her left leg partially paralyzed. Doctors warned that she might never walk again without a brace. However, Wilma's family refused to let this prognosis define her life.

Every week, Wilma's mother drove her 50 miles for physical therapy at a college for black people only, since local hospitals were segregated and didn't offer the same level of care. At home, her siblings took turns massaging her weakened leg, all contributing to her recovery. This relentless support from her family fueled Wilma's determination, and by age twelve, she defied medical expectations by removing her leg brace and taking her first independent steps.

The transition from those tentative steps to international stardom began in high school when a track coach noticed her speed. Despite her frail health, Wilma's resolve led her to train rigorously, often running around the school's basketball court and on the local dirt tracks. Her dedication paid off dramatically at the 1960 Rome Olympics, where she became the first American woman to win three gold medals in a single Olympiad. Her races were a marvel of speed and grace; she dominated the 100 meters, 200 meters, and the 4x100 meter relay, earning her the nickname "The Tennessee Swift." Each stride on the Olympic track was not just a move toward victory but a leap toward changing the perception of African-American and female athletes worldwide.

Wilma's Olympic success was a watershed moment in sports and the context of the Civil Rights Movement. It was a time when African Americans were fighting for basic civil rights. Wilma's victories, much like Jesse Owens's 24 years earlier, served as a potent symbol of African American capabilities and the potential for gender equality in sports. Her triumphs were celebrated across racial divides, providing a narrative that contradicted the prevalent discriminatory ideologies of the time. She became a living testimony to the power of resilience and ambition, irrespective of the racial and gender prejudices that tried to hinder her path. Her media appearances and interviews further amplified her role as an advocate for civil and women's rights, using her platform to champion the causes of equality and integration.

Post-Olympics, Wilma's influence extended beyond the racetracks. She retired from amateur athletics shortly after her Olympic victories and focused on promoting education and sports. Recognizing the transformative power of education from her own life, Wilma completed her degree. She worked in various community service roles, from coaching at her alma mater, Tennessee State University, to working in youth outreach programs. She understood that her legacy would be the records she set and the paths she paved for future generations of athletes, especially girls who dreamed of running their own races.

Rudolph's commitment to nurturing young talent often brought her into schools and community centers, where she shared her story and encouraged children to pursue their dreams with the same determination that helped her overcome polio and racial barriers.

Wilma Rudolph's story is a tale of overcoming adversity through sheer determination and the unwavering support of her family, who believed in her potential. From a child who was once told she might never walk to an Olympian who soared on the world stage, Wilma Rudolph remains a towering figure in the history of sport, inspiring all who hear her story to strive for their highest potential, no matter the odds.

CHAPTER 3
TERRY FOX

THE MARATHON OF HOPE

TERRY FOX, A VIBRANT TEENAGER FROM CANADA, LOVED SPORTS JUST LIKE YOU AND ME. However, at only 18, Terry faced something tougher than any opponent on the sports field: he was diagnosed with osteosarcoma, a type of bone cancer, which led to the amputation of his right leg above the knee. You would have thought Terry's sports journey ended there, but instead, it was just beginning…

Facing such a life-altering challenge, Terry could have stepped back. Instead, he laced up his shoes and decided to make a difference. With an artificial leg, Terry set a goal that seemed nearly impossible—he planned to run across Canada from coast to coast to raise awareness and funds for cancer research. His vision was clear: the Marathon of Hope. This wasn't just a run; it was a mission fueled by personal struggle and a deep desire to prevent others from enduring the same pain he experienced. His family, friends, and entire communities came together to support this daring dream. They helped organize the logistics, spread the word, and cheered him on, turning his personal challenge into a collective crusade against cancer.

On April 12, 1980, Terry dipped his prosthetic leg in the Atlantic Ocean and began his journey from St. John's, Newfoundland. Imagine starting such a daunting task, not just physically but emotionally. Every morning, Terry ran close to 42 kilometers. That's a marathon a day! A feat that even the fittest athletes would find grueling. He faced the physical pain of running on an artificial leg, the unpredictable weather, the vast and lonely roads, and the constant fatigue. Yet, Terry kept running.

As he made his way through the provinces, more and more people began to take notice. What started as a small ripple in Newfoundland became a wave of support and love across the country. Canadians lined up on the streets, at gas stations, and town halls to see the young man running for a cause much bigger than anyone. Media outlets started covering his journey, broadcasting the inspiring story of Terry Fox to the whole country and beyond. His determination and humble nature won the hearts of millions, and his daily run became a symbol of hope and perseverance.

Terry's Marathon of Hope lasted 143 days and covered over 5,300 kilometers. Although he had to stop near Thunder Bay, Ontario, because cancer had spread to his lungs, the impact of his marathon didn't fade. By February 1981, Terry Fox had achieved his goal of raising one dollar for every Canadian, totaling over $24 million. Today, the annual Terry Fox Runs are held in over 60 countries and have raised hundreds of millions of dollars for cancer research. His legacy is a testament to the idea that one person's efforts can indeed change the world.

Schools across Canada and around the globe teach students about Terry Fox's heroic efforts, ensuring his mission endures through generations. His story is not just about running; it's about facing life's toughest challenges with determination and hope. It's a reminder that no obstacle is too big when you have a heart full of courage and a world of supporters cheering you on.

Reading through Terry's journals and listening to his speeches, one can't help but be moved by his sincerity and genuine concern for others. Terry said in one of his reflections, "Even if I don't finish, we need others to continue. It's got to keep going without me." These words echo the selfless spirit with which he ran every kilometer. Canadians and people worldwide don't just see Terry Fox as a hero; they see him as a friend, a family member who stood up in the face of adversity and ran toward it with all his might. His story continues to inspire millions to believe that anything is possible when you dare to dream big and put your heart and soul into making it a reality.

His legacy is not just in the funds raised or the kilometers run, but in the spirits lifted, the communities united, and the lives forever changed by his extraordinary journey.

CHAPTER 4
LESSONS FROM THE LEGENDS

JESSE OWENS

STAND TALL IN THE FACE OF ADVERSITY. NO MATTER HOW TOUGH THINGS GET, ALWAYS BELIEVE in your ability to succeed. Jesse proved that determination can overcome prejudice, showing the world that greatness isn't defined by where you come from, but by how you rise above challenges.

WILMA RUDOLPH

Nothing is too difficult. Even if the odds seem stacked against you, with enough heart, you can achieve greatness. Wilma, who once couldn't walk without braces, became the fastest woman on earth, reminding us that our past does not dictate our future.

TERRY FOX

Inspire others through your actions. Sometimes, your courage and determination can make a difference far beyond your own life. Terry's Marathon of Hope showed that even when life seems unfair, you can turn your struggle into a beacon of hope for millions.

CHAMPIONS OF THE RING

CHAPTER 5

MUHAMMAD ALI

MORE THAN A BOXER

MUHAMMAD ALI WAS NOT JUST A PHENOMENAL BOXER; HE WAS A SHOWMAN, A POET, AND A provocateur. His ability to charm the public was as powerful as his punches. From his early days as Cassius Clay (he changed his name later on in life), Ali was known for his witty rhymes and bold predictions, often proclaiming himself "The Greatest" long before the world acknowledged it. His charisma wasn't just surface-deep; it was a crucial part of his identity that drew people to him inside and outside the sports world.

Ali's flair for dramatics and his sharp tongue made every interview and pre-fight weigh-in a spectacle. He used rhymes and catchy phrases to psych out his opponents and engage with the media and fans. This unique blend of humor, confidence, and intelligence made Ali a favorite among sports journalists and a role model for many. His charismatic leadership extended beyond his words; it was reflected in his actions, his way of treating people, and his ability to turn every fight into a story worth telling.

At the height of his career, Muhammad Ali made a decision that would redefine his legacy. In 1967, during the Vietnam War, Ali refused to be drafted into the military, citing his religious beliefs and opposition to American involvement in Vietnam. "I ain't got no quarrel with them Viet Cong," he famously said, a statement that resonated across a divided America. His refusal cost him dearly—Ali was stripped of his heavyweight title, faced a five-year prison sentence (though he remained free while appealing), and was banned from professional boxing during his prime years.

Ali's stand against the Vietnam War positioned him as a symbol of civil resistance and a voice for the African-American struggle for justice and equality. His willingness to sacrifice his career and financial stability for his beliefs inspired many, but also attracted criticism and anger from various segments of society. This chapter in his life is a stark reminder of the personal costs of standing up for one's convictions, but also of the profound impact such a stand can have on society.

Ali's influence extended well beyond the boxing ring. He was a crucial figure in the Civil Rights Movement, using his fame to speak out against racial injustice and support movements that fought for equality and human rights. Ali's ability to speak boldly and eloquently about issues of race and inequality made him a controversial figure, but also a powerful agent of change. His advocacy went beyond speeches; it was reflected in his everyday interactions and his refusal to be subdued by societal expectations of athletes, especially black athletes.

In his later years, Ali's focus shifted from confrontation to reconciliation and humanitarian efforts. He served as a United Nations Messenger of Peace, traveling to countries affected by poverty and conflict, such as Afghanistan and North Korea, to promote humanitarian efforts and provide aid. His work with the Make-A-Wish Foundation and his Muhammad Ali Parkinson Center highlighted his commitment to helping others, regardless of their background or circumstances.

Ali's humanitarian efforts were driven by his strong convictions and understanding of the global platform his sports career provided him. Whether delivering medical supplies or helping negotiate the release of hostages, Ali was deeply involved in his missions, often putting himself in complex and sometimes dangerous situations to help those in need. His global outreach helped redefine what it means to be a sports hero, showing that the true measure of greatness lies in the ability to impact the world positively.

Muhammad Ali's story is more than just a tale of a boxing legend. He wasn't just the greatest in the ring; he was the greatest in life. His battles were fought not only against opponents but against injustice and inequality. Ali's refusal to be drafted into the Vietnam War, despite the personal cost, showed that he valued his principles more than his titles. His words, "I am the greatest," weren't just about his boxing skills—they were about his belief in the power of standing up for what's right. Ali's legacy is one of courage, not just in fighting, but in speaking out. His life teaches us that a true champion is someone who fights for others, not just for themselves. As you read about his life, think about the kind of impact you want to have on the world. Let his life inspire you to think beyond the ring, beyond the game, and towards a greater purpose. Remember, as Ali once said, "Service to others is the rent you pay for your room here on earth."

Scan the QR code to watch a video of Muhammad Ali in action!

CHAPTER 6
LAILA ALI

KEEPING IT IN THE FAMILY

STEPPING INTO A WORLD DOMINATED BY THE TOWERING LEGACY OF HER FATHER, MUHAMMAD, Laila Ali carved her own niche in the boxing ring with a blend of grace and grit that is all her own. Imagine the weight of expectation when your father is known as "The Greatest." Yet, Laila did not just follow in Muhammad Ali's footsteps—she created her own path, and with each step, she redefined what it means to be a female athlete in a sport long ruled by men.

From a young age, Laila was drawn to sports, but it wasn't until after she graduated that she first donned boxing gloves. The decision wasn't easy. The boxing world was, and to some extent still is, a male-dominated sport where female boxers often fought more for recognition than titles. Laila, however, saw this as a challenge rather than a barrier. Her determination to succeed was fueled by personal ambition and a desire to honor her father's legacy while forging her own identity.

Her boxing debut came in 1999, and she quickly rose through the ranks, winning numerous fights with a combination of skillful technique and powerful punches. Her undefeated record speaks volumes—24 wins with no losses, including 21 knockouts.

Her achievements inside the ring are only part of her story. Laila's success helped shine a spotlight on women's professional fighting, generating more fans for boxing and increasing acceptance in the broader sports community. She was winning respect for female boxers everywhere, showing they could draw crowds and headline events like their male counterparts.

One particularly memorable moment in her career came when she fought Jacqui Frazier-Lyde in 2001. It was billed as "Ali/Frazier IV," a nod to their fathers' famous trilogy. The fight highlighted the legacy of two of boxing's greatest families and the rise of women in the sport. Laila won by a majority decision after eight rounds, but the real victory was for women's boxing, which enjoyed unprecedented attention and respect following the fight.

Beyond the ring, Laila Ali has been a vocal advocate for women's rights and empowerment. She has used her public platform to speak out on issues affecting women, particularly in sports. Her advocacy extends to encouraging women to take up space in all areas of life, whether in athletics, business, or personal development. Laila's efforts have inspired countless young girls to pursue their dreams with conviction, no matter the obstacles.

After retiring from boxing in 2007, Laila redirected her energy into various endeavors that reflect her passions and values. She has authored books, hosted TV shows, and engaged in speaking engagements, all focusing on themes of health, wellness, and motivation. Her work as a fitness expert is particularly notable, combining her sports experience with her commitment to healthy living.

Laila's philanthropic efforts are also a significant part of her post-boxing life. She has been involved in numerous charitable activities, focusing on children's nutrition and women's health issues. Through these efforts, Laila continues to impact the world positively, leveraging her fame to support and uplift others. Her journey in and out of the ring teaches us about the power of heritage and the importance of creating one's legacy. As Laila herself has shown, the fight for equality and recognition is ongoing, but with perseverance and passion, barriers can be broken.

CHAPTER 7
LESSONS FROM THE CHAMPIONS

MUHAMMAD ALI

SPEAK UP FOR WHAT YOU BELIEVE IN. YOUR VOICE MATTERS, AND STANDING UP FOR YOUR beliefs can change the world. Ali's refusal to be silenced made him not just a champion in the ring but also a hero for justice, teaching us that true strength comes from conviction.

LAILA ALI

Break barriers. Don't let anyone tell you that you can't achieve something because of who you are or where you come from. Laila carved her own path in a male-dominated sport, showing that with confidence and hard work, you can forge a legacy of your own.

HEROES ON WHEELS

CHAPTER 8
BRADLEY WIGGINS

CYCLING PRODIGY

BRADLEY WIGGINS IS A LEGEND ON TWO WHEELS, A TRAILBLAZER WHO REDEFINED WHAT WAS possible in cycling. With his unmistakable sideburns and mod-inspired fashion, Wiggins became a household name in the UK, not just for his style but also for his extraordinary achievements, which made him a legend in the world of sport.

Born to a family with cycling in its blood, Wiggins' journey to greatness began at an early age. As a young boy in London, he dreamed of becoming a champion, and it wasn't long before his natural talent began to shine. His early success on the track caught the cycling world's attention, and he became known for his incredible speed, endurance, and strategic mind.

Bradley Wiggins believed in "Marginal Gains." That meant making many small improvements that would make a big difference in his performance. He paid close attention to every little detail, like how much sleep he got, what he ate, and even how his bike was set up. By focusing on these tiny things, Wiggins showed incredible discipline, always looking for ways to improve, even if it was just a little bit.

To get ready for the rugged mountain climbs in the Tour de France, Wiggins would spend weeks training alone in high-altitude mountains. Every day, he'd wake up early, ride his bike up steep hills, and stick to a strict routine. Even though it was exhausting and sometimes lonely, Wiggins knew that pushing himself this way would make him stronger for the races ahead. Wigging also pushed himself to be as healthy as possible, following a very strict diet, often eating the same plain foods every day. He sometimes even ate by himself to avoid being tempted by other foods. This showed his determination to stay focused on his goals, even when it meant making tough choices.

Wiggins trained on the Isle of Man, where the weather was often windy and rainy. Instead of avoiding the bad weather, he embraced it, riding his bike through rainstorms and strong winds. Wiggins believed that facing these challenges in training made him mentally tougher and better prepared for anything that could happen during the Tour de France.

And it was on the roads of France in 2012 that Bradley Wiggins truly made history, achieving something no British cyclist had ever done before—winning the prestigious Tour de France. The Tour de France is often described as the most grueling and challenging race in the world, a test of physical and mental strength that pushes riders to their absolute limits. For years, it seemed like an impossible dream for any British cyclist to conquer this epic race.

Winning the Tour de France was a monumental moment for British sport. Wiggins' victory wasn't just a personal triumph but a victory for a nation that had long been overshadowed in the world of cycling. Wiggins shattered the barriers, proving that British cyclists could compete—and win—on the biggest stage. His success inspired a new generation of cyclists, showing them that no dream is too big, and no challenge is too great if you dare to pursue it.

But Wiggins' impact on the sport didn't stop at the finish line. He went on to win five Olympic gold medals, making him Britain's most decorated Olympian at the time. His versatility as a cyclist—excelling in both track and road racing—set him apart as one of the greatest all-around cyclists in history. His achievements will likely stand the test of time, as few have matched his ability to dominate in such diverse disciplines.

Beyond his victories, Wiggins has also been a powerful advocate for mental health. He has spoken openly about the pressures and challenges faced by athletes, breaking the stigma around mental health issues and encouraging others to seek help when needed. His honesty and bravery in addressing these topics have made him a role model, not just for his athletic achievements, but for his willingness to use his platform to make a difference.

After retiring from professional cycling, Wiggins didn't ride off into the sunset. Instead, he continued contributing to the sport he loves, sharing his insights as a commentator and analyst, and inspiring future generations through his autobiography and public speaking. He also dedicates time to charitable work, promoting cycling and healthy living, ensuring that his legacy goes far beyond his time on the bike, and helping others with their mental and physical health.

CHAPTER 9

MICHAEL SCHUMACHER

SPEED KING

MICHAEL SCHUMACHER IS MORE THAN A FAMOUS FIGURE IN FORMULA 1 RACING – HE'S A TRUE icon. Dubbed the "Speed King," Schumacher made a lasting impact on the world of motorsport by shattering records and setting standards that may stand the test of time. His focused and strategic racing style made him a tough competitor on the track.

Beyond racing, Schumacher was known for his approachable nature and ability to connect with fans and the media, earning him admiration not just as a racer but as a beloved personality in motorsport. His friendly demeanor helped bridge the gap between Formula 1's high-energy environment and fans worldwide, solidifying his legacy as a significant figure in the sport.

Schumacher's journey began in Germany, where, as a young boy, he fell in love with racing. His father, a kart track manager, helped him get his start in karting, a type of motorsport that's often the first step for future F1 drivers. From the moment he got behind the wheel, Schumacher showed a natural talent for speed. He won race after race, quickly making a name for himself as a rising star.

However, Schumacher's success wasn't just due to his natural talent. He was known for his incredible work ethic and attention to detail. Every aspect of his racing was meticulously planned. He studied every track, learned every corner, and analyzed all of his performances to ensure he constantly improved. Schumacher's approach to racing was similar to Wiggin's "marginal gains" style—he believed that making many small improvements would lead to big results. Whether it was adjusting his driving technique, fine-tuning his car's setup, or working on his physical fitness, Schumacher left no stone unturned.

One of the things that made Schumacher stand out was his ability to stay calm under pressure. Racing at speeds over 200 miles per hour, with other cars inches away, requires nerves of steel. Schumacher was known for his mental toughness. He could focus entirely on the race, blocking out distractions and staying cool even in the most intense situations. This mental strength was one of his greatest assets, allowing him to make split-second decisions that could mean the difference between winning and losing.

Training was also a massive part of Schumacher's success. He didn't just rely on his natural ability—he worked tirelessly to stay in top shape. Schumacher was one of the first drivers to bring a new level of physical fitness to Formula 1, understanding that being in peak physical condition would give him an edge on the track. His training was grueling, including long hours in the gym and on the track, pushing his body to its limits. This dedication to fitness set a new standard in the sport, inspiring future drivers to follow his example.

And inspiring others is perhaps his biggest legacy. In 2000, he joined Ferrari, a team that had not won a championship in over twenty years. Many thought it was impossible for them to win again. But Schumacher believed in the team, and through hard work and determination, he helped lead Ferrari to five consecutive World Championships. His success brought the team back to the top of Formula One and cemented his place as one of the greatest drivers of all time.

Even after retiring from racing, Schumacher's influence continued to expand. Schumacher made donations to various charities and actively participated in humanitarian initiatives. He demonstrated that being a champion transcends track achievements—it also involves leveraging success for the betterment of society.

Michael Schumacher's life took a tragic turn on December 29, 2013, when he was involved in a serious skiing accident in the French Alps. Since that day, he hasn't been seen in public, and his family has kept his condition private. Although we haven't seen him since that fateful day, Schumacher's impact will forever be etched in history as a model for achievement on the racetrack and in everyday life. His story will forever be about the power of focus and the importance of never settling for second best.

Scan the QR code to watch a video of Michael Schumacher in action!

CHAPTER 10

LESSONS FROM THE HEROES

BRADLEY WIGGINS

AIM FOR CONSISTENCY. SUCCESS ISN'T JUST ABOUT ONE BIG WIN; IT'S ABOUT PERFORMING WELL over time. Bradley's endurance on the track and road highlights the power of persistence and how small, steady steps can lead to historic achievements.

MICHAEL SCHUMACHER

Master your craft. Dedicate yourself to becoming the best at what you do through focus and hard work. Michael's precision on the racetrack, combined with relentless training, shows that excellence isn't accidental—it's earned through unwavering dedication.

WAVES OF COURAGE

CHAPTER 11

BETHANY HAMILTON

BEYOND THE ATTACK

ONE CRISP MORNING, A YOUNG BETHANY HAMILTON ENTERED THE WATERS OF KAUAI, Hawaii, to go surfing. She did not know that her life was about to change forever.

At just 13 years old, Bethany was attacked by a 14-foot tiger shark, a terrifying encounter that resulted in the loss of her left arm. But what happened next is what truly defines her. Instead of succumbing to fear and despair, Bethany chose to face her new reality with an unbreakable spirit. Just one month after the attack, she was back on her surfboard, determined to pursue her passion for surfing.

The road to recovery was tough. Bethany had to relearn how to balance on her board and master the waves with one arm. Every day presented new challenges, both physical and mental. She had to adapt her surfing techniques and find new ways to maintain balance and control in the water. Her family and community rallied around her, providing the support and encouragement she needed to push forward. Bethany's resilience and determination became her hallmark, turning her story into one of the most inspiring comebacks in sports history.

In 2005, she won the National Scholastic Surfing Association (NSSA) National Championship, which is a big deal because it's where the best young surfers in the country compete. She also won the T&C Women's Pipeline Pro in 2007 and the Surf N Sea Pipeline Women's Pro in 2014, both of which are held at the famous Banzai Pipeline in Hawaii—one of the most challenging and respected waves in the world.

Bethany's triumphant return to surfing symbolized bravery amidst adversity. Her story captivated the global media, shining a spotlight not just on her incredible talent, but also on her undying courage. Bethany became an icon for disabled athletes, challenging the perceptions and boundaries of what was possible in surfing. Her presence in the sport encouraged a more inclusive environment, inspiring other surfers with disabilities to chase their dreams and embrace the waves without fear.

Her influence extended beyond the surfing community. Bethany's story was featured in numerous magazines, documentaries, and even a film, "Soul Surfer," which portrayed her journey from tragedy to triumph. She reached a global audience through these mediums, teaching people everywhere about the power of perseverance and the human spirit's capacity to overcome adversity.

Bethany's impact is not limited to her surfing achievements. She has become an influential advocate for ocean safety and the inclusion of disabled athletes in sports. Through public speaking engagements and her autobiographical books, Bethany shares her experiences and insights, promoting a message of safety, resilience, and empowerment. She juggles this with her roles as a wife, mother, and mentor to young surfers.

Bethany's journey is not just about winning competitions; it's about embracing every aspect of life with enthusiasm and grace. She continues to inspire young surfers, showing them that with passion and perseverance, they can overcome any wave of challenges that come their way—her story reminds us that true strength comes from the heart and that our setbacks can become our greatest comebacks.

Scan the QR code to watch a video of Bethany Hamilton in action!

CHAPTER 12
MICHAEL PHELPS

HUMAN FISH

MICHAEL PHELPS IS OFTEN CALLED "THE HUMAN FISH," AND FOR GOOD REASON. HE'S THE most decorated Olympian of all time, with an incredible 23 gold medals to his name! Let that sink in. Twenty. Three. Golds.

Phelps' journey to becoming the greatest swimmer in history was one of fierce determination and a deep love for the sport that kept him pushing forward, even when the odds were against him.

Phelps was born in Baltimore, Maryland, and his relationship with water began at the tender age of seven, initially as a means to channel his overflowing energy and manage his ADHD.

ADHD stands for Attention-Deficit/Hyperactivity Disorder, and people who have it may have trouble focusing, may act impulsively without thinking, and may be more physically active than is typical for their age.

Phelps's ADHD worked in his favor. The pool became his sanctuary, a place where he could sharpen his focus and unleash his potential. Under the guidance of coach Bob Bowman, Phelps adopted a rigorous training regimen that included grueling daily practices, even on holidays. His commitment was total, and his life was structured around maximizing his swimming capabilities. Each Olympic cycle saw Phelps enhancing his technique and adding to his skill set, carefully selecting events that maximized his medal potential. His strategic approach to choosing events was not just about tallying victories but about pushing the limits of human performance.

Having ADHD meant focusing outside the pool was challenging, yet he turned it to his advantage by channeling his hyperfocus into training. He trained harder than anyone else, often swimming six hours a day, six days a week. He followed a strict routine that included swimming laps, weight training, and practicing his technique until it was flawless. Phelps believed in the power of repetition, knowing that every lap he swam brought him one step closer to perfection. This level of dedication is what sets him apart from other athletes.

While Phelps found it hard to focus outside of the pool, one of the things that made him unique was his ability to stay focused in the pool, even under the immense pressure of the Olympic Games. He developed a mental routine that helped him block out distractions and keep his mind sharp. Before every race, Phelps visualized himself swimming in the perfect race, going over every stroke in his mind. This mental preparation allowed him to stay calm and confident, even when the stakes were at their highest.

Phelps was also known for his incredible endurance. To prepare for the demanding schedule of the Olympics, where he would sometimes compete in multiple events on the same day, Phelps would push his body to its limits during training. He would swim long distances at top speed, forcing his body to adapt to the intense physical demands. This grueling training regimen gave him the stamina to dominate race after race, day after day, Olympics after Olympics.

Phelps also inspired others to dream big and work hard. At the 2008 Beijing Olympics, he achieved the seemingly impossible by winning eight gold medals in a single Games, breaking the record set by fellow American swimmer Mark Spitz. This incredible feat wasn't just a personal triumph—it was a moment that captured the world's imagination, showing that with determination and hard work, even the most unreachable goals could be achieved.

The mental weight of this expectation took its toll, however, leading Phelps to confront serious challenges, including battles with depression. These struggles were intensely personal battles fought in the public eye, adding layers of complexity to his career and personal life. Yet, Phelps's story is also one of transformation and redemption. Through acknowledging his mental health struggles, he opened up important conversations about the pressures athletes face. His comeback, marked by a historic performance at the 2016 Rio Olympics after a brief retirement, was not just a return to the sport but a statement about resilience and the human capacity to overcome.

Phelps revolutionized swimming techniques, most notably with his underwater dolphin kick, often referred to as the "Phelps Kick." This technique, which involves propelling the body using a dolphin-like movement of the legs, became his secret weapon. It is a testament to his innovative approach to swimming that swimmers worldwide have adopted this technique, changing the way athletes swim at butterfly and freestyle events. Phelps's ability to master and modify his technique underlined his understanding of water dynamics, making him a pioneer in competitive swimming.

Even after retiring from competitive swimming, Phelps has continued to make a difference. He has become a strong advocate for mental health, using his platform to discuss the importance of seeking help and breaking the stigma around mental health issues. Phelps' openness about his own struggles has inspired many people to take care of their mental health, just as they would their physical health.

Phelps's legacy is one of triumph, adversity, innovation, and advocacy. As a swimmer, he set a benchmark for excellence that may remain unmatched for generations. His journey teaches us that greatness is achieved not just in the spotlight but in the countless hours of effort behind the scenes. As a human being, he showed that even Olympians are not immune to life's struggles and that true strength lies in the ability to face one's vulnerabilities and emerge stronger.

CHAPTER 13
LESSONS FROM THE ATHLETES

BETHANY HAMILTON

EMBRACE YOUR UNIQUE JOURNEY. YOUR CHALLENGES CAN BECOME YOUR GREATEST strengths. After losing her arm to a shark, Bethany didn't just return to surfing—she became a symbol of resilience, teaching us to ride the waves life throws at us.

MICHAEL PHELPS

Set your own records. Compete with yourself and strive to be better today than you were yesterday. Michael's numerous Olympic medals are proof that continuous self-improvement can lead to extraordinary success, far beyond what others might expect.

DEFYING THE ODDS

CHAPTER 14

JIM ABBOTT

A ONE-HANDED WONDER IN BASEBALL

JIM ABBOTT PLAYED MAJOR LEAGUE BASEBALL—NO BIG DEAL, RIGHT? THOUSANDS OF PEOPLE have done that. But how many people do you know who did it with one hand?!

Hailing from Flint, Michigan, Jim Abbott was born without his right hand and faced a pivotal choice early on: view his disability as a roadblock or embrace it as another challenge to conquer. Supported by his family, who refused to treat him differently or limit his potential, Jim was encouraged to participate in sports like any other child. With their unwavering backing, Jim not only took part but thrived, particularly in baseball and football. His high school baseball coach devised innovative methods to cater to his unique circumstances, enabling Jim to seamlessly switch his glove between his residual limb and left hand after pitching so he could field effectively.

Abbott's hard work and dedication paid off. After excelling in high school, he earned a spot on the University of Michigan's baseball team, where he became a standout pitcher. His incredible talent and perseverance caught the attention of major league scouts, and in 1989, he was drafted by the California Angels—straight out of college. What made this even more remarkable was that Abbott skipped the minor leagues entirely, a rare feat in baseball.

But Abbott's success wasn't just about his unique pitching style. He was known for his fierce determination and never-give-up attitude. Even in the face of tough competition, he remained calm and focused, believing that he could always find a way to win. His teammates admired his work ethic, often saying that Abbott worked twice as hard as anyone else, ensuring his one-handed technique was flawless.

One of the most amazing moments in Abbott's career came on September 4, 1993, when he pitched a no-hitter for the New York Yankees against the Cleveland Indians. A no-hitter is one of the rarest achievements in baseball, where the pitcher doesn't allow a single hit from the opposing team. This incredible feat proved that Abbott wasn't just a good pitcher—he was one of the best. This accomplishment, which many pitchers can only dream of, was made even more impressive by Jim's perceived 'disadvantage.' His performance that day inspired millions, showing them that no obstacle is too great to overcome.

In classrooms and sports programs nationwide, Jim's story is used to teach important lessons on diversity, overcoming challenges, and the significance of inclusivity. His ability to transcend conventional ideas about disability has established him as a renowned athlete and positioned him as a key figure in the ongoing conversation about equality in sports.

Jim Abbott's connection with fans, especially young athletes navigating their disabilities, is arguably his biggest legacy. Through interactions like meet-and-greets, baseball clinics, and social media engagement, Jim has actively reached out to inspire and guide the upcoming generation of athletes. His friendly demeanor and willingness to share his experiences have endeared him to baseball enthusiasts and communities advocating for disability rights and inclusivity.

His consistent participation in different projects ensures that his message of strength and empowerment remains a source of inspiration and motivation. He demonstrates that heroes are not just fictional characters; they exist in our everyday lives, guiding us on how to lead boldly and with intention.

CHAPTER 15

DEREK REDMOND

UNFORGETTABLE OLYMPIC FINISH

DEREK REDMOND WAS A BRITISH RUNNER WHO DAZZLINGLY DOMINATED THE ATHLETICS world in the late 1980s and early 1990s. Unbelievable achievements marked his sprinting career, but he will be mostly remembered for one event.

As a young athlete, Derek quickly made a name for himself on the track, showcasing his speed and, most importantly, his resilience. His journey was challenging, as injuries repeatedly tested his resolve. But Derek's determination never wavered. He repeatedly kept coming back stronger from every injury setback. And there were plenty.

In 1992, with injuries seemingly a thing of the past, he hit his peak form. It seemed inevitable that he would win gold at the upcoming Barcelona Olympics. The stage was set for one of the most heart-wrenching yet inspiring moments in sports history.

Derek's participation in the 1992 Olympics was not just another competition; it was a culmination of years of grueling training and recovery from numerous injuries that would have ended many athletes' careers. As he lined up for the 400m semi-final race, the excitement and tension were palpable. Derek started strong, his form flawless as he rounded the track. But fate had a cruel twist in store. Mid-race, a sharp pain shot through his hamstring. He had just torn one of the biggest muscles in his leg. A debilitating injury that saw him collapse on the track. But what happened next turned a moment of agony into an unforgettable symbol of perseverance.

Refusing to stay down, Derek struggled to his feet, determined to finish the race he had trained so passionately for. What followed was a scene that would be etched into the memories of everyone who witnessed it. Derek's father, Jim Redmond, ran onto the track, past security, to his son's side. Together, father and son made their way around the track, Derek leaning on Jim for support, his face etched with pain and determination. The crowd rose in a standing ovation, moved by the sheer willpower and love that unfolded before them. Derek did not win the race, but he won the hearts of millions worldwide, embodying the true spirit of the Olympics in a way that was as inspirational as any other victory seen at the Olympics.

The emotional impact of that semi-final race transcended the boundaries of sport. Derek Redmond's refusal to give up in the face of near-insurmountable pain captured the essence of true perseverance. This moment became one of the most memorable in Olympic history, not for a record set or a medal won, but for its profound display of human spirit and resilience. It reminded everyone that sometimes, true victory lies not in finishing first but in the courage to continue despite the odds.

Following his athletic career, Derek Redmond's influence continued to resonate. He turned to motivational speaking and sports psychology, drawing on his own experiences to inspire athletes and non-athletes alike. Derek's message is powerful—challenges and setbacks can be transformed into sources of strength. Through his speeches and work-shops, he has encouraged countless individuals to face their obstacles with courage and to never lose sight of their goals, no matter how distant they may seem.

Derek Redmond's legacy is defined by more than his athletic achievements; it is shaped by his character and impact on the world of sportsmanship. His career and that unforgettable Olympic moment have sparked discussions about the meaning of success and the qualities that define a true champion. In schools, sports clubs, and international platforms, Derek's story continues to inspire conversations about courage, resilience, and the importance of finishing what you start.

CHAPTER 16
LESSONS FROM THE ATHLETES

JIM ABBOTT

PLAY TO YOUR STRENGTHS. EVEN IF YOU FACE PHYSICAL LIMITATIONS, THERE'S ALWAYS A WAY to excel. Born without a right hand, Jim pitched a no-hitter in the major leagues, proving that true talent lies in how you use what you have, not what you lack.

DEREK REDMOND

Finish what you start. No matter what happens, keep going until you cross the finish line. Derek's courageous limp to the finish line with his father's help shows that true victory isn't always about winning—sometimes, it's about the fight to finish.

MIRACULOUS TEAMS

CHAPTER 17
USA ICE HOCKEY TEAM 1980

THE MIRACLE ON ICE

IN THIS CHAPTER, WE DIVE INTO ONE OF THE MOST THRILLING AND INSPIRING TEAM STORIES IN sports history—the 1980 US Hockey Team. The story is known as "The Miracle on Ice," and its protagonists caused one of the greatest upsets in sports history. The story beautifully embodies teamwork, determination, and belief in the impossible. This American team redefined what was possible in ice hockey, proving that any underdog can come out on top with heart and grit.

The year is 1980, and the world is deep in the Cold War, a period of intense rivalry between the United States and the Soviet Union not just in terms of military might but in the domains of science, space, and, yes, sports. The Olympic Games, held in Lake Placid, New York, became more than just a sporting event; they were a stage for ideological battle, where each victory was infused with greater meaning. Imagine the pressure on the athletes, where every game had the weight of national pride and global politics resting on it.

The US hockey team, composed mainly of college players, was set to face the Soviet Union—four-time defending gold medalists and the undisputed powerhouses of ice hockey. The Soviets were professional players, seasoned and skilled, a team that had demolished the NHL All-Stars 6-0 in an exhibition match before the Olympics. In contrast, the young American team was not expected to stand a chance. The political tension of the era added a layer of intensity to the match, transforming it into a symbolic fight for national honor.

But the USA team had something special. They were a group of young men with a lot of heart and something to prove. Under the leadership of coach Herb Brooks, a man known for his brutal and innovative coaching style, the team focused on becoming a cohesive unit. Brooks pushed his players hard, knowing they couldn't rely on individual talent alone to take down the mighty Soviets. He believed in the philosophy of "conditioning, chemistry, and commitment," drilling his team endlessly until they played as one.

The team trained relentlessly, often in grueling conditions. Brooks was known for his infamous "Herbies," a punishing drill that had players skating back and forth across the rink until they were utterly exhausted. This grueling preparation wasn't just about physical endurance—it was about mental toughness. Brooks knew that to beat the Soviets, his team had to be stronger, smarter, and more resilient than ever before.

February 22, 1980, marked the day of the iconic game. The arena was charged with energy, the air thick with anticipation. The game started fast, with the Soviet team dominating early, as expected. However, under Brooks' guidance, the US team stuck to their game plan. They played a fast-paced and aggressive style, a stark contrast to the more structured and methodical Soviet play.

Key plays, such as Mark Johnson's game-tying goal with just one second left in the first period, kept the Americans in the game and built their confidence. The turning point came in the final period when team captain Mike Eruzione scored the go-ahead goal, putting the US team up 4-3. The crowd erupted, sensing that something miraculous was unfolding before their eyes.

The final minutes were a showcase of teamwork and determination, with the US team banding together to protect their slim lead against the relentless Soviet attack. When the final buzzer sounded, the impossible had been achieved. The US team had won, defeating the seemingly invincible Soviets in what would be called the "Miracle on Ice."

The 1980 US Hockey Team's victory had a lasting impact on American hockey and sports as a whole. It was a defining moment that showed the world that anything is possible with enough heart and teamwork. The players themselves became symbols of American pride and perseverance, their careers forever defined by that miraculous game.

The impact extended beyond the ice. This game was a morale boost for the United States, coming at a time when the country needed a win, both literally and metaphorically. It was a story that went beyond sports, touching the hearts of millions and reminding everyone that underdogs could triumph even in the face of significant obstacles.

The "Miracle on Ice" legacy is not just in the medals won or the game played but in the enduring belief that miracles can happen when people come together, united by a common goal. It remains a prime example of achieving the impossible through unity, strategy, and an indomitable spirit— the ultimate tribute to the enduring spirit of teamwork.

CHAPTER 18
LEICESTER CITY 2016

In 2015/2016, Leicester City Football Club kicked off their season in the English Premier League, with everyone thinking they would come last and be relegated to the second tier of English football. Everyone was so convinced that they would perform so poorly in a league that contained the world's best soccer stars that the odds of them *winning* the Premier League title stood at a 5000 to 1 figure. That meant that people thought Kim Kardashian running for the US presidency was more likely to happen than Leicester City winning the league.

What followed was one of the most remarkable underdog tales in sports folklore.

Leicester City's journey to glory didn't start with superstars or massive budgets. In fact, the club was one of the smallest in the Premier League, and they had narrowly avoided relegation the season before. Most people expected them to be fighting at the bottom of the table again. But Leicester had something that couldn't be measured in money or fame: they had heart, determination, and a belief that anything was possible.

The team was led by manager Claudio Ranieri, a man known for his calm and thoughtful approach. Ranieri wasn't just a tactician; he was a motivator, someone who knew how to get the best out of his players. He believed in building a team that worked together, where every player knew their role and gave their all for the group. Ranieri's philosophy was simple: work hard, stay humble, and never give up.

Leicester's success was built on these principles. The players trained relentlessly, focusing on the basics of the game: strong defense, quick counter-attacks, and relentless pressure. They didn't have the star power of teams like Manchester United or Chelsea, but they had something just as powerful: a deep understanding of teamwork and an unbreakable spirit.

One of the key players in Leicester's incredible season was Jamie Vardy, a striker who had worked his way up from the lower leagues. Vardy's story is one of perseverance. He wasn't a typical football superstar—he didn't come from an elite academy or have a glamorous background. But what he did have was an unstoppable drive and a knack for scoring goals. Vardy broke records that season, including scoring in 11 consecutive games, a Premier League record still in place. His pace and tenacity made him a nightmare for defenders and a hero to Leicester fans.

Another crucial figure was N'Golo Kanté, a midfielder with seemingly endless energy. Kanté was everywhere on the pitch, breaking up opposition attacks and driving his team forward. His tireless work ethic and incredible stamina were vital to Leicester's success. Alongside him was Riyad Mahrez, a creative genius who dazzled fans with his skill and vision. Mahrez's ability to unlock defenses and create chances for his teammates made him one of the season's standout players.

One unforgettable moment was when they clinched a 3-1 victory against Manchester City at the Etihad Stadium. It was a match where Leicester's swift counter-attacking approach flawlessly dismantled the team that was expected to win the league. Each Leicester City victory that followed after being Manchester City instilled confidence not just among the players but also among the fans and media outlets. The far-fetched dream started to take on the semblance of a plausible reality.

The climax of Leicester's story came on May 2, 2016, when they were officially crowned Premier League champions. They didn't even have to play that day— Tottenham Hotspur, the only team that could catch them, failed to win their match, and the title was Leicester's. The scenes of celebration were unforgettable: fans filled the streets, players danced in joy, and the football world stood in awe of what Leicester had achieved.

Leicester City's triumph wasn't just a victory on the pitch—it was a victory for the underdogs everywhere. They showed that even in modern sports, the most impossible dreams can come true with hard work, belief, and a bit of magic.

But Leicester's impact didn't end with their title win. Their success changed the way people thought about football. They proved that you don't need the biggest budget or the biggest stars to achieve greatness. What you need is a team that plays for each other, a manager who believes in them, and a never-say-die attitude.

The legacy of Leicester City's 2016 season will live on forever. They didn't just win a title—they redefined what was possible in soccer. Their story will be told for generations, inspiring young players and fans to believe in their dreams, no matter how impossible they might seem. Leicester City proved that in soccer, as in life, the underdogs can rise to the top and make history.

Scan the QR code to watch a video of Leicester City of 2016 in action!

CHAPTER 19
LESSONS FROM THE TEAMS

USA ICE HOCKEY TEAM 1980

BELIEVE IN THE IMPOSSIBLE. SOMETIMES, THE BIGGEST UNDERDOGS CAN ACHIEVE THE MOST incredible victories. The "Miracle on Ice" reminds us that with teamwork and belief, no challenge is too great, no opponent too strong.

LEICESTER CITY 2016

Teamwork makes the dream work. Success is sweeter when everyone works together. Leicester's Premier League victory was a testament to the power of unity, proving that a team with heart and harmony can achieve what seemed unachievable.

PERFECT 10 PERFORMANCES

CHAPTER 20

NADIA COMĂNECI

THE PERFECT SCORE

NADIA COMĂNECI IS MORE THAN A MERE NAME IN GYMNASTICS—SHE'S A HERO, A LEGEND, and an absolute superstar with an incredible tale to tell.

Nadia's journey to greatness began in Romania, where she discovered her love for gymnastics at a young age. Her natural talent was apparent early on, and she quickly caught the attention of coach Béla Károlyi, who recognized her potential and took her under his wing. Under his guidance, Nadia trained tirelessly, dedicating countless hours to perfecting her routines. She was known for her incredible work ethic, and she didn't just aim to be good—she aimed to be the best.

Growing up in Communist Romania also presented its unique set of challenges. The political and social landscape of the time placed significant pressure on athletes like Nadia, who were often seen as national symbols of pride and success. The expectations were sky-high, and the margin for error was minimal. Despite these pressures, Nadia's focus never wavered. Her training not only prepared her for the technical challenges of gymnastics but also instilled a resilience that would define her career.

One particularly poignant moment in Nadia's career came during a competition before the 1976 Olympics, where she performed despite suffering from a severe flu. Weak and dizzy, Nadia chose to compete, driven by personal ambition and a sense of duty. Though not perfect, her performance was a testament to her grit and determination. These qualities, coupled with her extraordinary talent, prepared her for her Olympic triumphs and endeared her to fans around the world.

One of the most unforgettable moments in sports history happened in the summer of

1976 during the Olympic Games in Montreal. At just 14 years old, Nadia executed an exceptional routine on the uneven bars and cemented her place in history.

As she landed gracefully, the crowd erupted in cheers. They eagerly looked at the scoreboard, awaiting the result of the beautiful routine they had just witnessed. There was a collective gasp when the scoreboard displayed a baffling "1.00." How could that graceful show have earned a 1.00?!

People in the crowd soon realized what was happening. The scoreboards had never been programmed to display a perfect 10.00—they had never needed to before Nadia's historic performance on that fateful day.

This groundbreaking achievement did more than earn Nadia a perfect score; it shattered the belief that perfection in gymnastics was unattainable. Her routine, marked by flawless precision and effortless grace, set a new standard in the sport. The impact was immediate and profound, resonating far beyond the gymnastics community. Nadia became an overnight sensation; her name was synonymous with excellence, and her performance symbolized achieving the impossible.

Behind Nadia's historic success was a testament to her hard work. The discipline she showed was immense. Everything she had done from a very young age — the hours at the gym, refining her techniques, building strength and flexibility — paid off that summer in Montreal. Her performance had a lasting impact on women's gymnastics, transforming how the sport was perceived and practiced globally. Following her performance, there was a noticeable shift in how female gymnasts were trained and choreographed. Emphasis on technical precision, artistic expression, and the overall aesthetic of the performance became more pronounced. Gymnastics routines became more complex and innovative, pushing athletes to new heights of excellence.

Nadia's success also inspired countless young girls to take up gymnastics, expanding the sport's popularity and accessibility. She became a role model for aspiring gymnasts, and her legacy is a beacon of what can be accomplished with talent and hard work. The evolution of gymnastics post-1976, with more countries investing in training programs and facilities, can be traced back to the global influence of Nadia's performances.

After retiring from competitive gymnastics, Nadia Comăneci did not quit the sport she loved. Instead, she embraced her role as an ambassador of gymnastics, promoting the sport across the globe and participating in various charitable activities. Her defection to the United States in 1989 marked the beginning of a new chapter, one where she used her fame to advocate for healthy lifestyles and youth sports participation.

Nadia's contributions to gymnastics are enduring, not just in the records she set but also in her ongoing efforts to inspire and nurture the next generation of gymnasts. Through clinics, speeches, and her charitable work, she continues to be a guiding force in the gymnastics community, and her life after the sport is as impactful as her time as a competitor.

CHAPTER 21

GREG LOUGANIS

DIVING TO GREATNESS

IMAGINE STANDING ON THE EDGE OF A HIGH DIVING BOARD, THE WATER BELOW A MIRROR, waiting to reflect your every move. Now, picture doing this with the grace of a dancer and the focus of a laser beam; this was how Greg Louganis approached diving, turning it into an art form. Known for his smooth and almost effortless dives, Greg's presence on and off the diving board blended calm focus and dogged determination. His ability to perform intricate dives with flawless execution made him a standout athlete in the world of competitive diving, earning him accolades and inspiring a generation to pursue the sport with passion and dedication.

In 1982, at the World Championships, Greg achieved something extraordinary. He became the first diver to receive a perfect score of 10 from all seven judges at a major international meeting, a feat that underscored his technical skill and artistic precision. This achievement was not just a personal milestone but a moment that raised the profile of diving worldwide, showcasing the sport's beauty and the heights of excellence that could be achieved. Greg's performance set new standards in diving, pushing the boundaries of what was considered possible.

Beyond that perfect 10, the climactic moments of Louganis' career came during the 1984 and 1988 Olympic Games, where he won gold medals in both the springboard and platform events, becoming the first diver to achieve this feat in back-to-back Olympics. But his path to victory in 1988 was far from easy. During the preliminary rounds, Louganis hit his head on the diving board while attempting a difficult dive, suffering a concussion. Most athletes would have been shaken, but Louganis showed incredible mental toughness. He returned to the board just minutes later, completing the dive and eventually going on to win gold. This moment became one of the most iconic in Olympic history, symbolizing the courage and determination that defined Louganis' career.

But Greg Louganis' legacy isn't just about his victories on the diving board—it's about his impact off it as well. In the years following his Olympic success, Louganis faced numerous challenges, including being diagnosed with a virus that was prevalent in the 1980s and 1990s and that many people mistakenly discriminated against. Instead of hiding from the world, Louganis chose to speak openly about his condition, becoming a powerful advocate for the awareness and education of the virus. His bravery in sharing his story helped to break down stigmas and inspire others facing similar challenges.

After retiring from competitive diving, Louganis continued contributing to the sport he loved. He became a coach and mentor, passing on his knowledge and experience to the next generation of divers. He also wrote a bestselling autobiography, "Breaking the Surface," where he shared his life story, including the struggles and triumphs that shaped him into the champion he became. Louganis' story has inspired countless people inside and outside the world of sports, showing that true greatness isn't just about what you achieve but how you use your success to make a difference.

Greg Louganis' legacy is one of excellence, courage, and resilience. His life story reminds us that being a champion isn't just about winning medals—it's about the journey, the obstacles you overcome, and the lasting impact you have on the people around you. Louganis will forever be remembered as a diving dynamo, a true legend who taught us that grace and grit can coexist, leading to extraordinary achievements.

CHAPTER 22
LESSONS FROM THE ATHLETES

NADIA COMĂNECI

Strive for perfection, but appreciate the journey. Excellence is about constant improvement, not just the final score. Nadia's perfect 10 in gymnastics taught us that while perfection is rare, the pursuit of it brings out our best, which can then help inspire others.

GREG LOUGANIS

Face your fears head-on. Being brave doesn't mean you're not scared—it means you do it anyway. Greg's triumphs in diving, even after a potentially life-changing injury, show that courage is about confronting what scares you and doing it anyway.

BASKETBALL BEASTS

CHAPTER 23

MICHAEL JORDAN

THE AIR UP THERE

MICHAEL JORDAN IS THE GREATEST BASKETBALL PLAYER OF ALL TIME. HE SINGLE-HANDEDLY shaped sporting culture worldwide and took basketball to unimaginable heights.

Born in Brooklyn, New York, and raised in Wilmington, North Carolina, Michael Jordan's journey wasn't always a straight shot to stardom. Picture a young Michael, full of energy and passion for sports, playing basketball in his backyard, dreaming of becoming a professional athlete one day. However, his path was met with hurdles right from the start. One of the most defining moments of his early career was not making his high school varsity basketball team on his first try. Instead of letting this setback defeat him, it fueled a fire within Michael, a determination to prove to his coach and the world that he had what it takes to be one of the greatest.

This early failure was a pivotal point for Michael. It taught him that success comes through perseverance and hard work. He spent hours practicing, honing his skills, and playing in junior varsity games, where he quickly became a standout player. His relentless dedication paid off when he finally earned a varsity spot and shone as a star player. This period of his life laid the foundation for his legendary work ethic and competitive spirit, traits that would define his career and inspire athletes around the globe.

After a stellar college career at the University of North Carolina, where he clinched the NCAA Championship with a game-winning shot, Michael Jordan was poised for greatness. Drafted by the Chicago Bulls in 1984, he quickly became a force to be reckoned with in the NBA. Michael's rookie season was marked by breathtaking performances that earned him the Rookie of the Year award, signaling the arrival of a new basketball icon.

Jordan's rise to NBA stardom was meteoric. His ability to score, agility, and precision made him a nightmare for defenders and a hero to fans. Throughout his career, Michael led the Bulls to many NBA championships, each victory further cementing his status as a basketball legend. His playoff performances were particularly spectacular, filled with buzzer-beaters and record-setting games that are etched in the annals of sports history.

One of the most memorable moments was "The Shot" in the 1989 playoffs against the Cleveland Cavaliers, where Michael, with the game on the line, leaped and scored the game-winning basket at the buzzer. This moment, among many others, highlighted his ability to perform under pressure, earning him the nickname "Air Jordan" for his seemingly gravity-defying leaps and unmatched air time.

The climactic moment of Jordan's career came during the 1990s when he led the Chicago Bulls to six NBA championships, including two three-peats (1991-1993 and 1996-1998).

Jordan's performances in the NBA Finals were nothing short of legendary. He was known for making clutch shots, like the iconic "Flu Game" in 1997, where he scored 38 points despite being severely ill. Moments like these solidified Jordan's reputation as the greatest of all time, a player who could always be counted on when the stakes were highest.

Michael Jordan was more than just a phenomenal athlete; he was a global icon who changed the face of sports marketing. His partnership with Nike led to the creation of the Air Jordan brand, a revolutionary line of sneakers that became a cultural phenomenon. The success of Air Jordan sneakers set a new standard for sports marketing, blending athletic performance with fashion and lifestyle, making Michael a household name worldwide.

Jordan's influence extended beyond the basketball court and into global markets, where he became a symbol of excellence and aspiration. His impact on the NBA's global popularity was profound, as he drew fans from all corners of the world, helping to transform basketball into a global sport. His legacy is not just in the records he set or the games he won but in how he inspired millions to strive for greatness, regardless of their field.

Off the court, Michael Jordan has left a lasting legacy through his philanthropic efforts and business ventures. His ownership of the Charlotte Hornets has allowed him to continue influencing the NBA. At the same time, his contributions to various charitable causes have shown his commitment to giving back to the community. Michael's influence also extends into popular media and fashion, where his status as a style icon continues to endure.

Through his Air Jordan Brand, a division of Nike, Michael has helped foster new talent in sports and beyond, supporting athletes, artists, and communities. His commitment to excellence and improvement resonates in his philanthropic work, which focuses on education, community building, and children's healthcare.

Michael's story is a reminder that greatness isn't handed to you; it's earned through hard work, sacrifice, and an unyielding desire to be better. He didn't just play basketball —he changed the game, setting a standard that athletes in every sport aspire to. Michael Jordan's legacy isn't just in the championships he won, but in how he inspired millions to believe that anything is possible with enough effort. His journey is a testament to the power of relentless ambition and the pursuit of excellence.

Scan the QR code to watch a video of Michael Jordan in action!

CHAPTER 24
LARRY BIRD

LET OUT OF THE CAGE

THIS CHAPTER SPOTLIGHTS LARRY BIRD, A PLAYER WHOSE NAME IS SYNONYMOUS WITH basketball greatness. Bird was a phenomenon who transformed the hardwood floors of the NBA into stages of legendary performances.

Picture a player who could stare down any challenge and turn the tide of any game with his sharpshooting skills. Known for his intense focus, Bird was a player who thrived under pressure, his eyes constantly scanning the court, mind calculating the next move. His competitive spirit was legendary, often seen in his fierce determination to outperform not just his opponents but also himself, game after game. Bird's trash-talking was part of his psychological strategy, a way to unsettle opponents while keeping his teammates fired up. Off the court, however, Bird was known for his down-to-earth nature, always approachable and ready to share a laugh, embodying the spirit of a true sportsman.

Larry Bird's journey is inspirational, from the small town of French Lick, Indiana, to the grand arenas of the NBA. Joining the Boston Celtics, Bird quickly became the team's cornerstone, leading them to three NBA championships and earning himself three consecutive MVP awards. His training regimen was as relentless as his playing style: hours spent practicing shots, studying opponents, and perfecting strategies. Bird's commitment to excellence saw him through numerous injuries and challenges, each time returning to the court with even greater resolve.

Bird's impact on basketball was profound, setting records that spoke of his versatility —career points, assists, and rebounds. But it was his ability to clutch victory from the jaws of defeat, making game-winning shots that seemed to defy possibility, that cemented his status as a basketball icon. For young athletes, Larry Bird's career is a testament to what can be achieved with hard work, dedication, and an unyielding desire to be the best.

The 80s was a decade dominated by his rivalry with Magic Johnson and the Los Angeles Lakers. This rivalry wasn't just about two players—it was about two teams, two styles of play, and two cities with a fierce competitive spirit. Bird led the Celtics to three NBA championships (1981, 1984, and 1986), earning two NBA Finals MVP awards in the process. His ability to perform under pressure, especially in clutch moments, made him one of the most feared players in the league. Whether hitting a game-winning shot or making a crucial pass, Bird's confidence never wavered, and he delivered when it mattered most.

One of the most defining moments of Bird's career came during the 1984 NBA Finals against the Los Angeles Lakers. In a crucial Game 5, with sweltering heat as the air conditioning in the Boston Garden had failed, Bird transcended the physical exhaustion and intense competition. He scored 34 points, leading the Celtics to a pivotal victory. This game, known as the "Heat Game," exemplified Bird's ability to perform at his best when the stakes were highest, showcasing his mental and physical toughness.

Beyond the basketball court, Larry Bird has been a champion for health and community development. His contributions have gone far beyond his hometown, extending to various health and youth-oriented initiatives. Bird has used his public platform to advocate for better health facilities and programs, especially in rural areas, understanding that access to good health care can significantly impact communities.

After his playing days, Bird took on roles as a coach and executive, influencing new generations of players and helping to shape the future of basketball. His involvement in charitable activities, particularly those aimed at improving community health and supporting local organizations, has shown his commitment to giving back to the community that supported him throughout his career.

To further engage with his legacy and learn from his incredible career, young athletes are encouraged to participate in the Larry Bird Challenge. This interactive element involves practicing specific basketball drills that Bird used during his career, helping young players improve their shooting accuracy, defensive skills, and overall game strategy. By participating in this challenge, young athletes develop their skills and connect with the history of basketball, understanding the discipline and dedication required to excel.

Larry Bird's story is a testament to the power of dedication, enthusiasm, and genuine love for basketball. It shows how an individual can transcend humble beginnings to become a revered figure worldwide. His impact goes beyond statistics and awards, resonating through the communities he has contributed to nurturing.

CHAPTER 25

KAREEM ABDUL-JABBAR

KAREEM ABDUL-JABBAR REDEFINED WHAT IT MEANS TO BE DOMINANT ON THE BASKETBALL court. Known for his signature shot, the "skyhook," Abdul-Jabbar became one of the greatest players in NBA history, setting records that have yet to be broken. But his story isn't just about scoring points—it's about intelligence, perseverance, and using his platform to make a difference in sports and society.

Abdul-Jabbar's journey in basketball is marked by relentless dedication and an insatiable desire to excel. With six NBA championships and six MVP awards to his name, his career is a testament to his hard work and exceptional skill. Kareem's training regimen was rigorous, and his dedication to mastering his skyhook set him apart from his peers. This dedication paid off in numerous aspects of his game, setting records for career points, blocks, and field goals and establishing him as one of the greatest players in the history of the sport. His ability to maintain a high performance throughout his long career is a testament to his physical prowess and mental discipline, making him a symbol of excellence and perseverance in basketball.

Kareem's legacy includes a particularly memorable game during the 1980 NBA Finals, where, despite an ankle injury, he put on a performance that is still talked about today. Scoring 40 points against the Philadelphia 76ers, he demonstrated not just skill but immense heart, pushing through pain to lead his team, the Los Angeles Lakers, to a crucial victory. This game was a defining moment in his career, showcasing his ability to overcome physical limitations with mental and emotional strength.

Beyond the basketball court, Kareem Abdul-Jabbar has been a vocal advocate for social justice, civil rights, and education. His intellectual nature shines through in his writing and public speaking, where he addresses complex social issues with depth and insight. Through his public image, he has supported educational programs and promoted cultural understanding, often focusing on the importance of education in achieving social change. His commitment to these causes is driven by a belief in using one's success to positively impact the world, a principle that has guided much of his life after basketball.

Kareem's post-playing career has been as dynamic as his time in the NBA. He has served as a coach, an author, and a cultural ambassador, roles that have allowed him to shape the future of basketball and influence the broader cultural landscape. His charitable efforts, particularly those to support youth programs and educational initiatives, reflect his commitment to giving back to the community. Whether mentoring young athletes or advocating for social justice, Karean continues to be a guiding force, promoting the sport of basketball and the values of equity and education.

CHAPTER 26
THE GAME CHANGERS

LESSER-KNOWN STORIES IN BASKETBALL

IN THE SHADOWS OF GIANTS LIKE MICHAEL JORDAN, THERE ARE PLAYERS WHOSE STORIES might not dominate the headlines but whose contributions have significantly shaped the world of basketball. One such pioneering figure is Chuck Cooper, who broke color barriers and paved the way for countless athletes. In 1950, Chuck became the first African American player drafted into the NBA, an event that marked a turning point in sports history. His entry into the league was not just about playing basketball but about challenging and changing the norms, showing that talent knows no color. Cooper's career, though not filled with flashy stats, was instrumental in integrating the sport, setting a precedent that the NBA would continue to build upon.

But the evolution of basketball isn't just about the players; it's also about the minds behind the moves - the coaches. Consider Red Auerbach, an architect of modern basketball, whose innovative strategies led the Boston Celtics to nine NBA championships. Auerbach was more than a coach; he was a visionary who introduced the concept of the sixth man, transforming the role of bench players in the game. Then there's Gregg Popovich, known affectionately as 'Pop,' whose leadership of the San Antonio Spurs has been marked by a focus on team unity and international scouting, bringing talents from around the globe to the forefront of the NBA, thus diversifying and enriching the league.

Amidst these strategic masterminds, there are countless players whose journeys speak volumes about resilience and determination. Like the story of Hansel Enmanuel a player who, despite losing an arm in a tragic accident as a child, has not given up on his NBA dreams. His adaptation and mastery of playing with one arm, as well as his ability to shoot and defend, not only earned him a place in the Northwestern State college basketball team but also served as a profound source of inspiration for people facing similar challenges. His story, though not widely known, underscores the extraordinary ability of human beings to adapt, overcome, and excel, inspiring us all with his unwavering determination. Very much a la Jim Abbott, who we saw in Chapter 14.

The global impact of basketball is another narrative enriched by players from all corners of the world. Dirk Nowitzki, a towering figure from Germany who took up basketball when he was only 13, brought international attention to the NBA with his unique playing style and sportsmanship. His success opened doors for other international players, showing that talent can come from anywhere and change the game in unexpected ways. Yao Ming's entrance into the league marked a significant moment for China and Asia. His impressive career with the Houston Rockets not only made him a star in the NBA but also a beloved figure in his home country, helping to skyrocket the popularity of basketball in Asia. These stories underscore the global reach of basketball, connecting us all through the love of the game.

These stories, from Chuck Cooper's groundbreaking draft to the strategic innovations of Auerbach and Popovich and the inspiring journeys of players overcoming adversity, weave together a rich tapestry of basketball history that extends far beyond the well-trodden path of its most famous stars. They remind us that every player and every coach contributes to the legacy of the game, influencing not just how basketball is played but also how it is perceived around the world.

CHAPTER 27
LESSONS FROM THE BEASTS

MICHAEL JORDAN

EMBRACE FAILURE AS A STEPPING STONE. MISTAKES ARE NOT THE END; THEY ARE LESSONS THAT make you stronger. Michael's missed shots didn't define him—his willingness to learn from them did, leading him to become a basketball legend.

LARRY BIRD

Lead by example. True leadership comes from your actions, not just your words. Larry's quiet determination on the court showed that greatness is about consistency and doing the right thing, even when no one is watching.

KAREEM ABDUL-JABBAR

Stay curious and never stop learning. Knowledge is power both on and off the court. Kareem's intellectual pursuits alongside his basketball career remind us that wisdom enhances talent and that true champions never stop learning.

VOLLEYBALL VIRTUOSOS

CHAPTER 28

WILFREDO LEÓN

A VOLLEYBALL PHENOMENON

WILFREDO LEÓN IS ONE OF THE GREATEST VOLLEYBALL PLAYERS TO HAVE EVER GRACED PLANET Earth.

Also known as "The Cuban Missile" because of his powerful spikes and explosive play, León is a young athlete whose name has become synonymous with volleyball excellence around the globe.

Wilfredo León's story begins in Santiago de Cuba, where he was born into a family with a volleyball legacy—his father being a former player. It was no surprise then that volleyballs surrounded Wilfredo as he took his first steps. By the age of seven, he was already playing the sport, and it wasn't long before his extraordinary abilities began to shine. His leap into volleyball stardom started early; at just 14, he made his debut for the Cuban national team, setting the stage for a career that would defy the norms of what young athletes are expected to achieve.

León's impact on the Cuban national team was immediate and profound. His incredible vertical leap, powerful serves, and sharp instincts on the court made him a pivotal player in international competitions. He helped lead the Cuban team to gold medals in several NORCECA Championships and a silver medal in the World League. These feats not only showcased his skill but also his ability to perform under pressure. His performances were so impactful that he quickly became the face of Cuban volleyball and a source of national pride for everyone on the island. Imagine being a teenager and already carrying the hopes of your country on your shoulders, jumping and spiking the volleyball with the same intensity and passion that you might put into your favorite video game or sport.

CHAPTER 29

KINGS AND QUEENS OF THE VOLLEYBALL COURT

RALLYING SUCCESS STORIES

IN THE WORLD OF VOLLEYBALL, CHAMPIONS COME FROM EVERY CORNER OF THE GLOBE, bringing with them unique styles, groundbreaking techniques, and stories of incredible perseverance. These athletes have not only mastered the game but have also used their platform to push the sport to new heights and inspire a whole new generation of players.

One such story is that of Giba, a legend of Brazilian volleyball. Known for his explosive power and strategic mind, Giba's influence on the sport extends beyond his multiple Olympic medals. He was instrumental in popularizing volleyball in Brazil, a country now known for its passionate fans and world-class teams. Giba's ability to perform under pressure was legendary, turning crucial points into spectacular displays of skill and determination. His knack for reading the opponent's setup and making split-second decisions made him a tactical genius on the court. However, his most significant contribution was his role in popularizing the libero position in volleyball, demonstrating its critical importance in modern defensive strategies. His career is filled with memorable matches that showcased his leadership and changed how teams approached the game strategically.

Then there's the inspiring story of Kerri Walsh Jennings from the USA, who, alongside her teammate Misty May-Treanor, dominated women's beach volleyball for over a decade, winning three Olympic gold medals. What makes Walsh's journey even more remarkable is that her last gold medal clinched in London in 2012, came while she was pregnant with her 3rd child. She not only proved that athletes can continue to compete at the highest levels as they balance family life but that winning gold is possible while carrying a little person inside you! Her resilience and dedication have made her a role model for athletes, especially women, demonstrating that personal and professional achievements do not have to be mutually exclusive. Walsh Jennings' ability to overcome physical and societal expectations has paved the way for future generations of female athletes to pursue their careers without compromise.

In volleyball, the synergy between players can often lead to unexpected victories, highlighting the importance of teamwork and leadership. An excellent example of this is the Japanese women's national team, known as "The Witches of the Orient." Under the leadership of coach Daimatsu, whose training methods were as innovative as they were strict, the team achieved a miraculous gold at the 1964 Tokyo Olympics. Their success was not just about individual skill but about how effectively they played as a unit, their movements synchronized, and their strategies perfectly executed. This historic win elevated the profile of volleyball in Japan and demonstrated the power of meticulous planning and collective effort in achieving sporting success.

The evolution of volleyball is also a story of technological and tactical advancements. Innovations in training methodologies, changes in the rules, and improvements in equipment have continually transformed how the game is played. Players like the Russian giant Dmitriy Muserskiy, standing at over seven feet tall, have changed the dynamics of the sport. His ability to use his height to deliver powerful spikes and blocks has led teams to seek taller players, shifting the focus toward more physically imposing lineups. Additionally, introducing the rally scoring system and the libero player were pivotal changes that have made the game faster and more exciting for players and fans alike.

As we explore these stories of diversity, adversity, teamwork, and innovation, we see that volleyball is more than just a game; it's a platform for expressing talent, overcoming challenges, and inspiring others, no matter where you come from or what obstacles you face.

CHAPTER 30
LESSONS FROM THE VIRTUOSOS

WILFREDO LEÓN

ADAPT TO EVERY SITUATION. BEING FLEXIBLE AND OPEN TO CHANGE WILL HELP YOU SUCCEED in any environment. Wilfredo's success in volleyball across different leagues and countries shows that adaptability is a key ingredient in achieving success.

KERRI WALSH JENNINGS

Kerri Walsh Jennings teaches us the power of partnership. Throughout her career, she demonstrated that working in perfect harmony with others can lead to incredible success. Alongside her partner, Misty May-Treanor, Kerri won three Olympic gold medals, showing that trust, communication, and teamwork are the keys to reaching the top.

GOLF GREATS

CHAPTER 31
ANNIKA SÖRENSTAM

DRIVING THROUGH BARRIERS

THIS CHAPTER TEES OFF WITH THE STORY OF ANNIKA SÖRENSTAM, A GOLFER WHO BROKE barriers and set records that rewrote the history of women's golf. Known as "The Queen of the Greens" for her incredible precision and consistency, Her journey from a young Swedish girl with a dream to one of the greatest golfers of all time reshaped the future of many young female golfers who would follow in her footsteps.

Born in Bro, Sweden, Annika swung her first golf club at the relatively late age of 12, setting her on a path to unprecedented success. Her journey from the rolling hills of Sweden to the manicured greens of the LPGA Tour was fueled by an unwavering commitment to excellence and a passion for the game that knew no bounds.

Sörenstam's passion paid off when she earned a golf scholarship to the University of Arizona, where she quickly became one of the top players in college golf. After turning professional in 1992, she steadily rose through the ranks as the accuracy with her irons was unrivaled. Her calm, focused demeanor on the course made her a household name within months. Sörenstam's commitment to practicing every detail of her game—whether it was perfecting her swing, mastering the greens, or maintaining peak physical fitness—set her apart from other players.

One key aspect of Sörenstam's success was her ability to stay calm under pressure. Golf is a game of precision; even the slightest mistake can have enormous consequences. But Sörenstam's mental toughness allowed her to perform at her best when it mattered most. She believed in the power of preparation and approached every tournament with the same intensity and focus, no matter the stakes.

Imagine the scene: it's 2001, and Annika is standing on the tee box at the Standard

Register PING tournament in Phoenix, Arizona. What happened next would go down in golf history. Annika shot a 59, becoming the first woman to break 60 in an official LPGA Tour event. This wasn't just a record; it was a statement. With every birdie, she chipped away at the doubts and limitations placed on female golfers, showing that they could achieve just as much, if not more, than their male counterparts.

The hero moment of Sörenstam's career came in 2003 when she made history by becoming the first woman in 58 years to compete in a men's PGA Tour event, the Bank of America Colonial. Although she didn't win the event, her courage and skill in competing against the best male golfers in the world inspired millions. This moment wasn't just about breaking gender barriers—it was about showing that with enough determination, you can compete at the highest level, no matter who you are.

Annika's impact on the world of golf extends beyond her scores. She won 10 major championships and a staggering 72 LPGA tournaments, numbers that tell the story of a dominant athlete. But Annika's influence was felt off the course as well. Her success challenged the perceptions of women in golf, encouraging countless young girls to pick up a club and aspire to the heights she had reached. She showed that with talent and determination, the fairways and greens were places where women could excel and lead.

Annika's career coincided with a transformative era in women's golf. Her presence and success helped increase the visibility of the women's game, attracting more spectators, sponsors, and media attention. This wasn't just good for the sport; it was revolutionary. Under her influence, prize money increased, tournaments were broadcast more widely, and more opportunities opened up for female golfers worldwide.

But Annika's contributions weren't limited to her playing days. She has been a fervent advocate for women's golf, working tirelessly to grow the game through the Annika Foundation, which promotes female participation in golf at all levels. Through her foundation, Annika has organized tournaments, clinics, and events designed to inspire the next generation of female golfers. Her commitment to nurturing young talent ensures that her legacy will influence the sport long after her retirement from professional play.

Annika's unique engagement with fans is one of the most distinctive aspects of her career. Recognizing the importance of her role as a model for young athletes, Annika has always made time to connect with her supporters, particularly young girls, encouraging them to pursue their dreams in golf and beyond. Annika Sörenstam's story is a reminder that sometimes, being a pioneer means taking risks and stepping outside of your comfort zone. She didn't just win tournaments; she inspired a generation of female athletes to aim higher and believe in their potential.

Scan the QR code to watch a video of Annika Sörenstam in action!

CHAPTER 32
TIGER WOODS

THE BEST

IMAGINE STANDING ON THE GREEN, THE CROWD SILENT, EYES FIXED ON YOU. WITH A STEADY hand and an intense focus, you swing your golf club, and the ball arcs beautifully before dropping into the hole. The crowd erupts, and you pump your fist, a signature move that fans worldwide recognize. This isn't just any golfer; this is Tiger Woods, a name that has become synonymous with golfing greatness. His calm demeanor under pressure, paired with a fierce competitive spirit, has made him a phenomenon in the world of golf.

Tiger Woods' approach to golf is marked by an intensity that transforms each tournament into a captivating display of skill and determination. Whether he's lining up a crucial putt or driving a ball down the fairway, Tiger's concentration is palpable. His ability to maintain composure and a fierce desire to win has often made the difference in tight matches. These qualities have defined his style of play and contributed significantly to his lasting legacy in the sport. His fist pump, a simple yet powerful gesture, has become a symbol of triumph, resonating with fans and aspiring golfers alike, embodying the thrill of victory and the personal satisfaction of overcoming challenges.

Tiger Woods entered the world golf scene in the 1990s when the sport was perceived as traditional and exclusive. This is a nice way of saying that Tiger was rarely welcome into any golf clubs to practice the sport he so deeply cherished. His emergence was not just refreshing—it was revolutionary. Tiger brought an unmatched level of athleticism and a new cultural perspective to golf. In 1997, at just 21 years old, he won the Masters Tournament by a record 12 strokes. This victory wasn't just a personal triumph but a historic moment for golf. Tiger's win shattered records and broke barriers, making him the first African American and youngest player ever to win the Masters. His performance captivated the world and signaled the beginning of a new era in golf, one where Tiger Woods would dominate like no one before him.

Over the next decade, Woods continued to rewrite the record books. He won 14 major championships, including multiple victories at the Masters, the U.S. Open, the British Open, and the PGA Championship. His incredible consistency, ability to perform under pressure, and relentless pursuit of excellence made him a fan favorite and the face of golf. Woods wasn't just winning tournaments—he was making them exciting, bringing millions of new fans to the sport and inspiring a new generation of golfers. He shattered records like there was no tomorrow, and by the age of 24, he had completed the Career Grand Slam, winning all four major championships—a feat that placed him among the greatest ever in the sport.

From a very young age, Tiger was introduced to golf by his father, and his connection to the game was profound. His training regimen was intense, involving both physical and psychological preparation. This early and continuous routine allowed him to handle the pressures of professional golf and to make a quick and indelible mark on the sport.

One of the most pivotal moments in Tiger's career came during the 2008 U.S. Open. Despite suffering from a severe knee injury, Tiger played through pain and delivered one of the most dramatic performances in golf history. In the final round, he needed a birdie to force a playoff. With the eyes of the world upon him, he made a staggering 12-foot putt that secured his position in the playoff, which he won the following day. This victory was not just about physical endurance; it showcased his mental toughness and relentless pursuit of excellence, traits that have defined his career.

Beyond the greens and fairways, Tiger Woods has used his influence to positively impact society, particularly in the field of education. Through the Tiger Woods Foundation, he has created unique learning experiences and scholarship opportunities for young people, focusing particularly on those from underprivileged backgrounds. His TGR Learning Labs offer innovative STEM curriculum and college-access programs, helping thousands of students gain valuable skills and knowledge.

Tiger's commitment to education reflects his belief in the transformative power of learning and his desire to give back to a community that did not always support him throughout his career—especially during the early days when racism was rife in the sport. These efforts underscore a fundamental aspect of his legacy—using his success as a platform to help others achieve their potential without going through the heartache that he did.

Following significant personal and physical challenges through the 2010s, Tiger's career experienced a remarkable resurgence with his win at the 2019 Masters. This victory, one of the greatest comeback stories in sports, highlighted his unwavering dedication and resilience. With golf being a sport in which you can succeed well into your senior years, the best of Tiger is probably yet to come…

CHAPTER 33
LESSONS FROM THE GREATS

ANNIKA SÖRENSTAM

BREAK NEW GROUND. DON'T BE AFRAID TO VENTURE INTO PLACES WHERE OTHERS HAVEN'T dared to go. Annika's decision to compete in men's golf tournaments showed that courage to break barriers opens doors for others to follow.

TIGER WOODS

Focus is key. In everything you do, concentration and attention to detail can set you apart. Tiger's dominance in golf came from an unparalleled ability to focus under pressure, teaching us that the mind is as powerful as the body.

SOCCER SULTANS

CHAPTER 34

LIONEL MESSI

THE GOAT

FROM THE HUMBLE STREETS OF ROSARIO, ARGENTINA, EMERGED A SOCCER PRODIGY WHO would one day be known as The Greatest Footballer of All Time. Lionel Messi's journey is a compelling testament to the power of humility and quiet confidence. Unlike many sports icons known for their flamboyant personalities, Messi's demeanor on and off the field has always been reserved, marked by a calmness that belies the intensity of his passion for the game.

Messi's trademark goal celebrations, often featuring a simple raise of his hands and a smile, reflect his understated approach to his achievements. Yet, beneath this calm exterior lies a fierce competitor driven by an unyielding desire to improve and succeed. This duality of quiet confidence and intense dedication has made Messi a phenomenal player and a source of inspiration for millions. His legacy extends far beyond the records he has shattered; it lies in the hearts of young fans and aspiring players who see in him a role model who combines incredible talent with genuine humility and sportsmanship.

Lionel Messi's football career is a combination of breathtaking moments and tonnes of records that might never be broken. From his early days at FC Barcelona, where he joined the famed La Masia academy at just 13, Messi's growth was propelled by more than just natural talent. Diagnosed with a growth hormone deficiency as a child, Messi's path was fraught with challenges that would have deterred many. But with the support of his family and the club, he not only overcame these challenges but also used them as fuel to propel his meteoric rise.

Throughout his career with Barcelona and the Argentine national team, Messi has accumulated an astounding array of titles and awards, including being an 8x winner of

the Ballon d'Or trophy. This is the trophy awarded by other footballers to the best footballer on the planet. No one else has come even close to winning this amount of Ballon
d'Or trophies. His record for the most goals scored for a single club captures the essence
of his dedication and loyalty to Barcelona, the team that stood by him from the beginning. Messi's impact on the field is matched by his symbolic importance as a beacon of
perseverance, inspiring aspiring athletes worldwide to pursue greatness against all odds.

One of the most defining moments of Messi's career came during the 2009 UEFA
Champions League semi-final against Chelsea. With everything hanging in the balance,
Messi demonstrated his skill and leadership under pressure. Though he did not score,
his assist in the dying minutes to Andrés Iniesta, who then scored the crucial goal, exemplified his ability to rise to the occasion. Fans and analysts often cite this match as a
turning point that cemented Messi's status as a skilled player and a clutch performer in
the most critical moments.

After almost 20 years of international heartbreak and not winning a trophy with his
country, Lionel Messi retired from international soccer. The world seemed set to lose a
soccer star at an early age, but luckily for us, Messi reversed his decision and led his
country to the Copa America of 2021.

At the 2022 World Cup in Qatar, Lionel Messi showed the world why he's undoubt-
edly the Greatest Footballer of All Time. Despite losing his first game against Saudi
Arabia, he led Argentina with incredible skill, scoring crucial goals at every tournament
stage, breaking down defenses with brilliant passes, and guiding his team through tough
matches. Messi scored twice in the final against France, and his calmness under pressure
helped Argentina win in a dramatic penalty shootout. His performance was nothing
short of magical, earning him the tournament's Best Player award and finally capturing
the World Cup trophy, completing his legendary career.

As Messi continues to write new chapters in his illustrious career with Inter Miami
FC, his role off the pitch is evolving. His involvement in football development programs
and his mentorship of young players at the Florida club exemplify his commitment to
nurturing the next generation of talent. His insights and experiences are invaluable
resources he is eager to share, ensuring that his legacy will influence the sport long after
hanging up his boots.

Messi's dedication to promoting football, mentoring young athletes, and advocating
for health and education reflects a holistic approach to his legacy. It's not about the spotlight or the fanfare, but about letting your actions speak for themselves. Messi didn't just
win trophies; he redefined what it means to be a team player, always putting the success
of his team above personal glory. Lionel Messi's legacy is a reminder that true greatness
often comes from humility, skill, and a deep love for the game. Remember that true
greatness usually lies in how you influence and uplift others around you.

CHAPTER 35
CRISTIANO RONALDO

THE PERFECT ATHLETE

IMAGINE THE STADIUM LIGHTS SHINING DOWN AS A FIGURE WITH UNMATCHED CHARISMA AND a magnetic presence charges down the football pitch. This is Cristiano Ronaldo, known for his skillful play and his dynamic personality that captures the heart of the sports world. Each of Ronaldo's games is a spectacle, not just because of his football prowess but also because of his passionate goal celebrations and natural leadership both on and off the field. His ability to inspire fans and teammates with his determination and skill makes *every* match memorable.

Ronaldo's journey in football reads like a script from a hero's tale. From his modest beginnings in Madeira, Portugal, he rose to become one of the greatest footballers of all time. His career has been adorned with numerous records and titles across Europe's top clubs, including Manchester United, Real Madrid, and Juventus, and he has had significant achievements with the Portuguese national team. His rivalry with Lionel Messi during the 2010s is legendary, each pushing the other to greater heights, captivating fans worldwide with their performances. Ronaldo's relentless training regimen and dedication to improving his game have seen him overcome challenges and continuously set new standards of excellence in football.

One of his most famous goals came for Juventus against Sampdoria, where Ronaldo jumped over two meters (higher than the defender marking him!) to head a goal for his Italian team. He also scored one of his most iconic goals against Juventus and playing for Real Madrid, a beautiful bicycle kick in the latter stages of the Champions League!

However, the most defining moments of Ronaldo's career came during the 2016 European Championship. In the final against France, despite suffering an early injury,

Ronaldo's presence and encouragement from the sidelines were pivotal, demonstrating his role as a leader, not just a player. His emotional investment and sheer will seemed to propel his team forward, culminating in Portugal's victory. This match underscored Ronaldo's importance to his team, not just for his on-field skills but for his ability to inspire and lead by example. For a few years, it also seemed like he'd be taking on the role of the Greatest Footballer of All Time before Messi went and got himself two Copa Americas and a World Cup!

Beyond the pitch, Ronaldo's impact is profound. His advocacy for health and fitness is well-known, with his social media often showcasing his rigorous training and diet routines. He uses his fame to encourage others to adopt healthy lifestyles, highlighting the importance of physical well-being. His humanitarian efforts are equally notable, including substantial donations to hospitals, particularly for children's health care, and his response to global crises, such as natural disasters, where he has contributed to relief efforts.

Ronaldo's commitment to excellence, health, and philanthropy, combined with his charismatic leadership, continues to inspire a new generation of footballers and fans. His legacy in soccer is not just about the goals scored or the titles won, but about the lives he has influenced and the standards he has set both on and off the field. His legacy is one of sheer determination and the belief that with enough hard work, dedication, and self-belief, you can achieve greatness, no matter where you start.

CHAPTER 36
LESSONS FROM THE SULTANS

LIONEL MESSI

LET YOUR ACTIONS SPEAK LOUDER THAN WORDS. SHOW YOUR TALENT AND DEDICATION through your work, not just by talking about it. Messi's humility, paired with his incredible skill, teaches us that true greatness is about letting your achievements do the talking.

CRISTIANO RONALDO

Always push your limits. Never settle; strive to exceed what you think is possible. Cristiano's relentless drive for self-improvement and peak fitness shows that success is about pushing past what others think is possible.

AMERICAN FOOTBALL GREATS

CHAPTER 37
TOM BRADY

THE ALL AMERICAN HERO

TOM BRADY IS THE MOST DECORATED QUARTERBACK IN NFL HISTORY. IF LIONEL MESSI IS THE soccer G.O.A.T., then there's no denying that his football equivalent is Tom Brady. Known for his ice-cool demeanor under pressure, Tom Brady's journey from a late draft pick to one of the greatest quarterbacks in NFL history is a tale of dedication, resilience, and a relentless pursuit of excellence.

Brady's journey to greatness began in San Mateo, California, where he grew up as a passionate sports fan, playing baseball and football. Despite his love for football, Brady wasn't a highly sought-after player in high school. He was often overlooked and had to fight for every opportunity to get noticed. When he finally got the chance to play college football at the University of Michigan, he spent much of his early career as a backup. Many would have perhaps given up at this point. But that word does not exist in Brady's vocabulary. Instead, he worked tirelessly to improve his game, showing the resilience and work ethic that would become his trademarks.

In 2000, Brady was drafted by the New England Patriots in the sixth round of the NFL Draft as the 199th overall pick— surely a position that meant a career-long backup. But Brady saw it differently. He saw it as his chance to prove himself. From the moment he arrived in New England, Brady focused on one thing: being the best. He studied the game relentlessly, spent hours perfecting his throws, and earned the trust of his coaches and teammates with his leadership and poise.

The most extraordinary moment of Brady's career came in 2001 when he stepped in as the Patriots' starting quarterback after an injury to the starter. Brady seized the opportunity and led the Patriots to their first-ever Super Bowl victory, defeating the heavily favored St. Louis Rams. This victory wasn't just a personal triumph but the beginning of a dynasty. Over the next two decades, Brady would lead the Patriots to nine Super Bowl appearances, winning six of them and adding another title with the Tampa Bay Buccaneers, making him the only player to win seven Super Bowls.

Of all the Super Bowls he contested, the most defining one of his career came during Super Bowl LI. That night, Tom Brady did something that had never been done before. With his team down 28-3 late in the third quarter, it looked like the game was over. But Brady didn't give up. He rallied the Patriots with brilliant plays, guiding them back from within the jaws of defeat. His passes were sharp, his decisions flawless, and he showed an unbreakable will to win. When the game finally ended, the Patriots had completed the greatest comeback in Super Bowl history, winning 34-28 in overtime. That night, Brady proved that no challenge was too big, and his legacy as the greatest quarterback ever was cemented. After that game, the world saw his ability to remain composed and focused in seemingly impossible situations.

His long list of accolades, including multiple NFL MVP awards and five Super Bowl MVP honors, underscores his standing as the jewel of quarterback excellence.

Beyond the gridiron, Tom Brady is a staunch advocate for health and wellness. His TB12 Method, which focuses on flexibility, diet, hydration, and mental fitness, reflects his holistic approach to health and longevity. Brady's commitment to maintaining peak physical condition has extended his career and inspired athletes across sports to consider how nutrition and lifestyle affect performance. By sharing his insights and routines, Brady encourages people everywhere to lead healthier lives.

Tom Brady's legacy is a testament to the power of believing in yourself and always being ready for your moment. To the man who created moments that will be remembered forever in football: We salute you, sir!

CHAPTER 38

JERRY RICE

HARD WORK PAYS OFF

JERRY RICE IS KNOWN FOR HIS METICULOUS WORK ETHIC AND A LASER-LIKE FOCUS AS A WIDE receiver. His career in the NFL is a testament to what passion and perseverance can achieve. Off the field, Rice's friendly demeanor and approachable nature made him a favorite among fans and a respected figure among his peers.

Rice's journey to greatness began in Starkville, Mississippi, where he grew up as one of eight children in a small, hardworking family. From a young age, Rice was introduced to the value of hard work, often helping his father, who was a brick mason. This early experience shaped his incredible work ethic, becoming the cornerstone of his success on the football field.

Despite his undeniable talent, Rice wasn't heavily recruited by major college programs. He ended up playing for Mississippi Valley State, a small school where he put up staggering numbers. By the end of his collegiate career, Rice shattered every Mississippi Valley State receiving record, catching 301 career passes for 4,693 yards and 50 touchdowns. That caught the attention of NFL scouts. In 1985, the San Francisco 49ers selected Rice with the 16th overall pick in the NFL Draft. From the moment he arrived in San Francisco, Rice was determined to prove he belonged among the best.

What set Rice apart was his physical ability and his commitment to always giving 100% of his effort into anything he did. He was known for his intense training regimen, constantly pushing himself harder than anyone else on the team. Rice's offseason workouts were the stuff of legend, involving long runs up steep hills and countless hours perfecting his routes and catching passes. He wasn't just training his body—he was training his mind, building the mental toughness that would allow him to perform under the most intense pressure.

The best moment of Rice's career came in the late 1980s and early 1990s when he helped lead the 49ers to three Super Bowl victories. Rice's performances in these championship games were nothing short of spectacular. In Super Bowl XXIII, he caught 11 passes for 215 yards and a touchdown, earning him the Super Bowl MVP award. His ability to come through in the biggest moments solidified his reputation as the greatest receiver in NFL history.

Rice's relentless pursuit of perfection extended to everyone around him. He demanded the best from himself, his teammates, and the rest of the staff at the 49ers. He inspired everyone around him to work harder and be better, from the quarterback to the kitman. Rice's dedication to his craft was unmatched and showed every time he stepped onto the field. Whether it was making an impossible catch, breaking a tackle, or outrunning defenders, Rice made it look effortless—but behind that effortlessness were countless hours of practice and preparation, a testament to his unwavering commitment to excellence.

One of the most inspiring aspects of Rice's career is his longevity. Even as he got older, Rice continued to perform at an elite level, setting a record of 1,549 receptions, and 22,895 receiving yards over his career in the NFL. The closest active player (as of 2023) is still thousands of yards away, making this record one of the most difficult to surpass. His ability to maintain such a high level of performance over two decades is a testament to his dedication and love for the game.

Jerry Rice's legacy is of excellence, discipline, and an unwavering commitment to greatness. He showed the world that being a champion isn't just about talent—it's about how much you're willing to put in to be the best. Rice's story reminds us that with hard work, determination, and a refusal to settle for anything less than your best, you can achieve greatness and inspire others to do the same.

Even today, Jerry Rice remains a symbol of what it means to be the best in football. His impact on the sport is still felt, and his name is synonymous with success, leadership, and the relentless pursuit of excellence. Rice's legacy as "The Greatest Receiver" will forever be remembered as a story of hard work, discipline, and the drive to be the best, inspiring football enthusiasts and athletes alike.

CHAPTER 39
LESSONS FROM THE GREATS

TOM BRADY

KEEP CALM UNDER PRESSURE. THE ABILITY TO STAY COOL AND FOCUSED WHEN THINGS GET tough is a true sign of greatness. Tom's ability to lead game-winning drives in the final minutes shows that composure is key to turning the tide in your favor.

JERRY RICE

Outwork everyone. Talent is important, but hard work is what separates the good from the great. Jerry's legendary work ethic and preparation remind us that while talent can start the journey, hard work is what completes it.

TENNIS TITANS

CHAPTER 40
ROGER FEDERER

ELEGANCE PERSONIFIED

ROGER FEDERER'S PRESENCE ON A TENNIS COURT IS ALMOST MAGICAL. KNOWN FOR HIS FLUID play and effortless grace, he moves with a poise that belies the intense focus and fierce determination driving each stroke. His calm demeanor during matches, a stark contrast to the intense energy of his play, has made him a favorite among fans, who admire his skill and sportsmanship. "The Maestro" became one of the greatest tennis players ever, setting records and captivating fans worldwide.

Federer's journey to greatness began in Basel, Switzerland, where he first picked up a tennis racket as a young boy. From the start, it was clear that Federer had something special. His natural talent was evident, but his relentless work ethic truly set him apart. Federer spent countless hours on the court, practicing his shots, perfecting his serve, and refining his footwork. He was determined to become the best and knew that talent alone wasn't enough—he needed to put in the work.

As Federer grew older, his skills developed rapidly. By the time he was a teenager, he was already being recognized as one of the top young talents in the world. But his rise to the top wasn't without challenges. Federer struggled with his temper early in his career, often letting his emotions get the better of him during matches. However, he soon realized that to achieve his full potential, he needed to control his emotions and stay focused. This turning point marked the beginning of Federer's transformation into the composed and focused champion the world would come to admire.

What set Federer apart wasn't just his physical ability but his elegance on the court. He played with a level of finesse that few could match, making even the most difficult shots look effortless. Federer's one-handed backhand became one of the most iconic shots in tennis, and his ability to glide across the court with such precision and grace earned him the nickname "The Maestro." His game was a perfect blend of power, speed, and technique, and he brought a level of artistry to tennis that had never been seen before.

The highlight of Federer's career came in the mid-2000s when he dominated the tennis world like no one else. Between 2004 and 2008, Federer won an astonishing 12 Grand Slam titles, including five consecutive Wimbledon championships and five consecutive U.S. Open titles. His rivalry with Rafael Nadal during this period produced some of the most memorable matches in tennis history, showcasing Federer's ability to compete at the highest level against the very best. In 2009, Federer surpassed Pete Sampras' record of 14 Grand Slam titles, cementing his place as the greatest of all time.

One of the most memorable moments during that era of dominance was the 2008 Wimbledon final, which is often called the greatest in tennis history. Facing his fierce rival Rafael Nadal, Federer displayed his top-tier skills and his heart, fighting back from the brink of defeat in a thrilling five-set match that captivated fans worldwide. Though he didn't win, his performance in this match is a highlight of his career, illustrating his resilience and his never-say-die attitude.

One of the most inspiring aspects of Federer's career is his longevity. Even as he grew older, Federer continued to compete at the highest level, winning Grand Slam titles well into his 30s, an age when most top players have already retired. His ability to adapt his game, overcome injuries, and stay motivated year after year is a testament to his dedication and love for tennis.

Roger Federer's legacy is one of elegance, excellence, and the pursuit of perfection. He showed the world that being a champion isn't just about winning—it's about how you win, with grace, dignity, and respect. Federer's story is a reminder that true greatness comes from within—from the dedication to improve every day, the ability to stay humble in victory, and the drive to be the best version of yourself.

Even today, Roger Federer remains a symbol of what it means to be a true champion in tennis. His impact on the sport is still felt, and his name is synonymous with success, sportsmanship, and the pursuit of excellence. Federer's legacy as "The Maestro of the Court" will forever be remembered as a story of grace and determination. He showed us that enduring champions carry themselves with dignity, regardless of the outcome.

Scan the QR code to watch a video of Roger Federer in action!

CHAPTER 41
NOVAK DJOKOVIC

THE SERBIAN EXPRESS

As we shift our focus from the calm and composed courts graced by Roger Federer, we meet another titan of tennis, whose fiery spirit and relentless pursuit of greatness present a compelling contrast. Playing in the same era as the dominant Federer and Nadal, this Serbian legend took tennis by storm and became the most decorated male player in the sport's history. His name? Novak Djokovic.

Known for his impassioned performances and no-nonsense personality, Djokovic has etched his name in tennis as the Greatest of All Time. If anyone were to argue this, he would just need to show his trophy cabinet to prove it. Djokovic's charisma on and off the court, coupled with a resilience that sees him fight for every point, inspires fans and fellow athletes alike. Djokovic isn't just playing; he battles, he entertains, and he connects, making each match an emotional journey for everyone watching.

Djokovic's ascent to the peak of tennis is a testament to his unyielding ambition and meticulous preparation. From his early years in war-torn Serbia, where he honed his skills in a drained swimming pool turned tennis court, Djokovic's journey has been a saga of conquering life's harshest challenges through sheer will and dedication. His record of 24 Grand Slam titles (as of August 2024) is a testament to his dominance, but it's his journey to these victories that truly defines his career. Each match showcases his never-give-up attitude, adapting play styles and mastering surfaces, from the clay of Paris to the hard courts of Australia, proving his versatility and tactical genius.

One of the most epic moments of Djokovic's career came in 2011, a year that saw him ascend to the very top of the tennis world. That season, Djokovic won three of the four Grand Slam titles— the Australian Open, Wimbledon, and the U.S. Open—along with a remarkable 43-match winning streak. His victory at Wimbledon, where he defeated Rafael Nadal, was the first time Djokovic claimed the world No. 1 ranking. This was not just a personal triumph—it was the moment when Djokovic solidified his place among the tennis greats and marked the beginning of the most outstanding male singles career in the sport.

His dogged determination to compete (and eventually overpass) the best two players ever seen in the sport came in the 2012 Australian Open final, where he faced off against one of those two men: Rafael Nadal. In a grueling match that lasted nearly six hours, Djokovic demonstrated not just physical stamina but immense mental fortitude. Battling through exhaustion and intense competition, his victory was a testament to his nickname, the "Iron Man of Tennis." This epic showdown is remembered for its length and for Djokovic's ability to maintain focus and resilience under extreme pressure, qualities that have defined his career. He beat Nadal and Federer in many other matches en route to becoming undisputed No. 1, seemingly always relying on his mental toughness rather than perhaps the more natural talent the other two greats possessed. Even at the grand old age of 37, Djokovic was making history by winning his first Olympic Gold medal at the Paris 2024 Olympics. It would seem that not even age would stop the tennis great.

Off the court, Djokovic's impact is equally profound. Passionate about health and well-being, he uses his platform to promote holistic health practices, emphasizing the importance of diet, mental health, and physical fitness. His struggles with dietary issues early in his career led him to adopt a gluten-free diet, a change that he credits with transforming his health and game. Today, Djokovic advocates for nutritional awareness, not just for athletes but for everyone, aiming to inspire healthier lifestyles through his example and initiatives. One of these initiatives is always having a hot glass of water and lemon first thing in the morning, as he claims it purifies all the toxins built up during his sleep.

Through the Novak Djokovic Foundation, the tennis star also champions early childhood education, particularly in his home country of Serbia. The foundation constructs preschools and enhances educational facilities, ensuring children can access quality education in a nurturing environment. His commitment to these causes showcases a star who is interested in winning trophies and uplifting communities, using his successes to open doors for others.

As we close this chapter on Novak Djokovic, we celebrate an athlete who embodies the spirit of mental toughness and generosity. It is a real-life story that shows us that skill isn't necessarily as important as the will to want to win, and that once you have reached the highest highs, the right thing to do is to continue showing the willingness to evolve, never forgetting to give back to those less fortunate. A true gentleman of the game.

CHAPTER 42
LESSONS FROM THE TITANS

ROGER FEDERER

BE GRACIOUS IN VICTORY AND DEFEAT. HOW YOU HANDLE WINNING AND LOSING DEFINES YOUR character. Roger's sportsmanship, whether winning or losing, teaches that dignity and respect for others are the true marks of a champion.

NOVAK DJOKOVIC

Keep evolving. Never stop improving and adding new elements to your game. Novak's ability to adapt and refine his skills over time shows that continuous evolution is key to staying ahead of the competition.

BASEBALL BEHEMOTHS

CHAPTER 43
BABE RUTH

THE GREAT BAMBINO

WHAT CAN YOU SAY ABOUT "THE COLOSSUS OF CLOUT," "THE KING OF CRASH," AND "THE Sultan of Swat" that hasn't been said before?!

Babe Ruth was more than just a baseball player; he was a showman, a trailblazer who redefined what it meant to be a powerhouse at the plate. His confidence and charismatic demeanor captivated fans and teammates alike.

Ruth's journey to greatness began in Baltimore, Maryland, where he grew up in a tough neighborhood. As a young boy, Ruth faced many challenges, and at the age of seven, he was sent to St. Mary's Industrial School for Boys, a reform school where he learned discipline and, most importantly, discovered baseball. At St. Mary's, Ruth's extraordinary talent was first noticed by Brother Matthias, a monk who coached the school's baseball team. Ruth's natural ability to hit the ball with power and precision quickly set him apart from the other boys, and it wasn't long before he earned a reputation as one of the best young players in the country.

Ruth's impact on baseball was revolutionary. He began his career as a pitcher for the Boston Red Sox, showing early signs of his versatility and talent. However, it was his batting that would redefine the sport. Ruth's approach at the plate was aggressive; his swings were powerful, and his home runs were record-setting. In an era when baseball was still finding its identity, Ruth's style of play injected excitement and a sense of spectacle into the game. He set numerous records, including his career home runs, RBIs, and slugging percentage, showcasing his skill and dedication to the sport. Every time Ruth stepped up to the plate, it was a potential history-making moment, and he seemed to thrive under that pressure, consistently delivering performances that are still celebrated today.

The best years of Ruth's career came in the 1920s when he was sold to the New York Yankees. This move marked the beginning of a new era in baseball, known as the "Golden Age," and Ruth was at the center of it all. In his first season with the Yankees, Ruth hit a mind-blowing 54 home runs, smashing the previous record and electrifying fans nationwide. His ability to hit home runs with such power and frequency changed the way baseball was played and viewed. Ruth's presence on the field wasn't just about winning games—it was about entertainment, excitement, and bringing a new level of energy to the sport.

One of the greatest stories from Ruth's career involved a young boy named Johnny Sylvester. In 1926, Sylvester was seriously ill, and Ruth promised to hit a home run for him in the World Series. True to his word, Ruth hit not one, but three home runs in Game 4, a feat that fulfilled a promise to a young fan and exemplified his flair for dramatic and heartfelt gestures. This story endeared Ruth even more to the public, highlighting his off-field kindness and ability to use his fame for good.

But Babe Ruth's impact wasn't just about the records and the accolades—it was about how he made baseball a national pastime. Ruth was a larger-than-life figure, both on and off the field, and his charisma and love for the game endeared him to fans of all ages. He wasn't just a baseball player—he was a cultural icon, someone who transcended the sport and became a symbol of the American Dream. He was a pioneer in turning athletes into celebrities. Ruth's story was one of rising from humble beginnings to achieve greatness, and it inspired millions of people who saw in him the possibility of achieving their own dreams.

One of the most remarkable aspects of Ruth's career is the lasting impact he had on the game of baseball. By the time he retired in 1935, Ruth had set numerous records, including 714 career home runs, a number that stood as the all-time record for nearly 40 years!

Babe Ruth showed the world that being a champion isn't just about talent—it's about using that talent to inspire others, to entertain, and to leave a lasting mark on the sport. Ruth's life as "The Sultan of Swat" will forever be remembered as a story of taking chances, embracing the spotlight, and having fun while doing it.

Scan the QR code to watch a video of Babe Ruth in action!

CHAPTER 44
WALTER JOHNSON

THE FASTBALL KING

IMAGINE STEPPING ONTO THE PITCHER'S MOUND, THE CROWD'S MURMURS TURNING INTO A hushed silence, all eyes on you as you wind up for the pitch. You do this with a quiet swagger, knowing you have the skill to outperform anyone, but you've been raised well enough to show grace in how you act. This type of humility is the kind that baseball player Walter Johnson, famously known as "The Big Train, " had.

Johnson wasn't just a fastball pitcher; he was a legend of sportsmanship and an example of integrity in the world of baseball. Off the field, he was equally admired for his quiet, humble demeanor and his approachable nature, making him a beloved figure among fans and a respected leader among teammates.

Johnson's journey to greatness began on a farm in Humboldt, Kansas, where he grew up working hard and developing the strength that would later make him a force on the mound. As a teenager, Johnson moved to California with his family, and it was there that he discovered his talent for baseball. Playing in local leagues, Johnson's fastball quickly became the stuff of legend. His pitches were so fast that catchers often complained of sore hands after catching for him, and batters struggled to even make contact with the ball.

In 1907, at just 19 years old, Johnson was signed by the Washington Senators, a team that would become his home for his entire 21-year career. From the moment he stepped onto the mound in the Major Leagues, it was clear that Johnson was something special. His fastball was practically unhittable, and his calm, unflappable demeanor made him a natural leader on the field. But what truly set Johnson apart wasn't just his speed—it was his control. He could place the ball exactly where he wanted it, making him a nightmare for opposing batters.

One of the most remarkable displays of Johnson's career occurred during a particularly challenging game against the mighty New York Yankees. With the bases loaded and the Senators clinging to a narrow lead, Johnson faced a lineup of heavy hitters. Instead of buckling under the pressure, he struck out three consecutive batters, using a mix of cunning sliders and his trademark fastball. This moment underlined his ability to perform under pressure and his strategic use of pitch selection, leaving fans and opponents in awe. Instances like these solidified his reputation as a reliable and formidable pitcher.

The hero moment of his time in baseball came in 1924 when he led the Senators to their first and only World Series championship. After years of playing for a team that often struggled, Johnson finally got the chance to showcase his talent on the biggest stage. In Game 7 of the World Series, Johnson came in as a relief pitcher in the ninth inning and shut down the opposing team for four scoreless innings, giving the Senators the chance to win in extra innings. This victory wasn't just a personal triumph—it was the crowning achievement of Johnson's storied career and a moment that solidified his place as one of baseball's all-time greats.

Johnson's dedication to the sport was evident in his relentless practice regimen and his consistent performance, which earned him 417 career wins—a testament to his perseverance and skill. What's more, Johnson's record of 3,509 strikeouts and 110 shutouts during his playing time showcased not just his ability to dominate batters but also his enduring stamina and strategic mastery on the mound.

Off the field, Walter Johnson was deeply committed to promoting sportsmanship and community involvement. He understood the platform his baseball fame provided and used it to influence positively. Throughout his life, Johnson was actively involved in various charitable activities, focusing particularly on youth sports programs and community development projects. His efforts to support local charities and his participation in events that promoted sports among children highlighted his belief in giving back to the community that had supported him throughout his career, inspiring others to do the same.

After retiring from active play, Johnson didn't leave baseball behind. He transitioned into roles that allowed him to continue shaping the sport, including coaching and managing teams. His stint as a manager for the Senators and later for the Cleveland Indians allowed him to impart his knowledge and values to a younger generation of players. His willingness to mentor young pitchers reinforced his commitment to the sport's future, and his desire to share his expertise made him a cherished figure long after his professional playing days ended.

In Johnson, we celebrate a man whose fastball was as legendary as his standard for what it means to be a true professional in the sport. His contributions to baseball continue to show that you don't need to boast to be recognized as one of the greatest, but that humility and dedication are the cornerstones of lasting success.

CHAPTER 45
LESSONS FROM THE BEHEMOTHS

BABE RUTH

DREAM BIG. SET YOUR SIGHTS HIGH AND DON'T BE AFRAID TO TAKE BIG SWINGS IN LIFE. BABE'S home run record came from his fearless approach to the game, teaching us that big dreams lead to big achievements.

WALTER JOHNSON

Stay humble. No matter how successful you become, always remember where you started. Walter's humility, despite being one of baseball's greatest pitchers, shows that true greatness is rooted in remembering your roots.

DRIVING LEGENDS

CHAPTER 46

JUAN MANUEL FANGIO

THE MAESTRO OF SPEED

ROARING ENGINES, FAST-PACED THRILLS, AND SPLIT-SECOND DECISIONS DEFINE THE WORLD OF Formula One racing. Juan Manuel Fangio was a man who could easily take all that in his stride. In fact, he raced with such grace and mastery that it earned him the nickname "El Maestro." This is the story of Juan Manuel Fangio, a legend whose calm demeanor and precise driving techniques set the standard in the golden era of auto racing.

Fangio's journey to greatness began in Balcarce, Argentina, where he grew up loving cars and speed. As a young man, he worked as a mechanic, learning the ins and outs of automobiles, which gave him a deep understanding of how cars worked. This knowledge would later become one of his greatest assets on the track. Fangio's racing career started in local events, where his natural talent quickly became evident. He was fast, but more importantly, he was smart—knowing when to push his car to the limit and when to conserve it for the long haul.

Fangio's big break came in the late 1940s when he began racing in Europe, the heart of international motorsport. Fangio's combination of speed, precision, and tactical brilliance set him apart from his competitors. By 1951, just a year after the inaugural Formula 1 World Championship, Fangio won his first title, driving for Alfa Romeo. But this was only the beginning of what would become a legendary career.

Fangio's career in Formula One is marked by an extraordinary record of five World Championships, a feat that made him the most successful driver of his time and set a benchmark that stood for decades. Arguably, the greatest moment of Fangio's career came in the mid-1950s when he dominated the sport like no one else. Between 1951 and

1957, Fangio won an incredible five World Championships, a record that would stand for nearly 50 years. What made Fangio's achievements even more remarkable was his ability to win with different teams—Alfa Romeo, Maserati, Mercedes-Benz, and Ferrari. He could adapt to any car, mastering its strengths and overcoming its weaknesses, which was a testament to his unparalleled skill and understanding of racing. His natural skill was outsmarting his competitors with superior racing know-how and impeccable timing.

One of the most iconic moments in Fangio's career occurred during the 1957 German Grand Prix at the Nürburgring, a race that many consider one of the greatest in the history of motorsport. Starting from pole position but falling 51 seconds behind due to a slow pit stop, Fangio demonstrated his exceptional skills by catching and passing the cars ahead of him in the final laps, setting fastest lap records several times in the process. In the final lap, he passed the race leader to take home one of the greatest victories ever seen in F1. This race underscored his reputation as a brilliant tactician and skilled driver and solidified his status as a legend of the sport. "Until that race, I had never demanded more of myself or the cars. But that day, I made such demands on myself that I couldn't sleep for two nights afterward," he said.

That year, Fangio was crowned the F1 driver with the highest career win percentage, 46.15%. An incredible figure that no other driver has ever come close to achieving.

Fangio personified focus and poise. His ability to remain calm under pressure allowed him to make strategic decisions that often led to spectacular victories, earning him the respect and admiration of fans and fellow drivers alike. His masterful control, tactical intelligence in races, and gracious personality contributed to a legacy that transcends generations.

One of the most remarkable aspects of Fangio's career is his enduring influence on the sport. Although his record of five World Championships was eventually surpassed by Michael Schumacher and Lewis Hamilton, Fangio remains the benchmark by which all other drivers are measured. His ability to win across different teams and cars and his consistent dominance in a dangerous era of racing set a standard of excellence that few have ever matched.

Beyond his achievements on the track, Juan Manuel Fangio was deeply committed to improving the safety standards in motor racing. During a time when racing was incredibly dangerous, Fangio used his influence to advocate for better safety measures, which helped to save lives and improve the sport. He was passionate about driver education and played a crucial role in mentoring young drivers, sharing his knowledge and experience to help them develop their skills.

After retiring from professional racing, Fangio remained active in the racing community, serving as a mentor, team advisor, and ambassador for the sport. He was instrumental in developing racing talent in Argentina and worked tirelessly to promote motorsport across the globe. Through his efforts, Fangio helped to foster a deeper appreciation for the technical and strategic aspects of racing, making the sport more accessible and enjoyable for fans and young racers worldwide.

CHAPTER 47

JIMMIE JOHNSON

SPEEDY JIMMIE

JIMMIE JOHNSON, OFTEN SEEN AS THE EPITOME OF DEDICATION IN THE WORLD OF NASCAR, has a personality that combines intense focus with remarkable sportsmanship. On the track, his driving is aggressive yet calculated, showing a deep understanding of the mind control needed to succeed in racing.

Off the track, Johnson is known for his approachable and humble nature; he regularly talks with fans and spends time with young racers, teaching them his craft. These qualities make him a champion and a true ambassador of NASCAR, inspiring fans and fellow drivers with his commitment to excellence.

Johnson's journey to greatness began in El Cajon, California, where he grew up loving motorsports. As a young boy, Johnson raced dirt bikes and off-road trucks, honing his skills on rough terrain and developing the mental toughness that would later make him a champion. His natural talent for racing was evident from an early age, but his dedication to pursuing his dream truly set him apart. Johnson knew that to succeed at the highest level, he would need to outwork and outthink his competition.

In 2002, Johnson made his full-time debut in the NASCAR Cup Series, driving for Hendrick Motorsports. From the moment he hit the track, it was clear that Johnson was a force to be reckoned with. He quickly made a name for himself with his smooth driving style and ability to stay calm under pressure. By 2006, just a few years into his career, Johnson won his first NASCAR Cup Series Championship. This victory began one of the most dominant runs in NASCAR history. By 2010, he had achieved the unprecedented feat of winning five consecutive NASCAR Cup Series Championships. This period of dominance was unlike anything the sport had ever seen, as Johnson consistently outperformed his rivals in every aspect of the race. He easily adapted to different tracks, weather conditions, and race strategies to make him unbeatable. Johnson's mastery of the "Chase for the Cup" format, which determined the season's champion, showcased his mental toughness and tactical brilliance. He knew when to go all out and when to play it safe, always keeping his eye on the ultimate prize.

A defining moment in Johnson's career that captured his spirit and skill occurred during a critical race at the Martinsville Speedway in Virginia. In the closing laps, Johnson executed a series of flawless maneuvers to take the lead and ultimately win the race. This victory was crucial in paving the way for one of his championship titles, demonstrating his knack for performing his best when the stakes are the highest, qualities that have made his career truly legendary.

Beyond the racetrack, Jimmie Johnson is a vigorous advocate for health and safety within the sport. Understanding the risks involved in racing, he has been a vocal supporter of initiatives to improve safety standards in NASCAR. Johnson's commitment extends to promoting wellness among drivers, emphasizing the importance of physical and mental health in achieving top performance. His involvement in developing safer racing technologies and practices has made a significant impact, helping protect drivers and ensure the sport continues to evolve positively.

Jimmie Johnson's legacy in NASCAR is one of resilience, innovation, and generosity. Through his achievements on the track and his contributions off it, Johnson continues to inspire future generations of drivers and anyone striving to excel in their pursuits. His career is a powerful reminder that with determination and a commitment to excellence, it is possible to leave a lasting mark not only in your field but also in the lives of others. Jimmie Johnson's career is a metaphor for how to live life, in that it's not how fast you go that is important, but how well you navigate the twists and turns along the way...

CHAPTER 48

LESSONS FROM THE LEGENDS

JUAN MANUEL FANGIO

PRECISION MATTERS. IN LIFE, PAYING ATTENTION TO THE SMALLEST DETAILS CAN LEAD TO THE greatest successes. Fangio's skill in racing came from his meticulous attention to every detail, teaching us that excellence is in the details.

JIMMIE JOHNSON

Pace yourself for the long haul. Life is a marathon, not a sprint; endurance is key. Jimmie's success in NASCAR came from his ability to maintain focus and stamina throughout long races, showing that patience and pacing are crucial.

HOCKEY HEROES

CHAPTER 49
WAYNE GRETZKY

THE GREAT ONE

WAYNE GRETZKY, A NAME THAT ECHOES THROUGH THE HALLS OF HOCKEY HISTORY, BEGAN HIS journey in Brantford, Ontario, where he first laced up his skates as a young boy. Known for his humble demeanor, Gretzky was never the loudest in the room, but his presence was always felt. His quiet confidence, much like that of Walter Johnson and Lionel Messi, who we saw a few chapters back, was inspiring for his teammates. These sporting G.O.A.Ts use their aura and skill to guide their teammates with a calm assurance that speaks louder than words.

By the time he was six, Gretzky was already playing against boys much older than him, and it was clear that he was an exceptional talent. His ability to see the game unfold, his quick hands, and his unmatched hockey sense set him apart from other young players. Even at a young age, Gretzky's understanding of the game was on another level—he didn't just play hockey; he seemed to think it.

At 17, Gretzky entered the World Hockey Association (WHA), and shortly after, he joined the NHL when the Edmonton Oilers merged with the league in 1979. From the moment he stepped onto NHL ice, Gretzky began rewriting the record books. His first full season in the NHL was a sign of things to come, as he won the Hart Trophy as the league's Most Valuable Player—a title he would go on to win eight consecutive times.

The ice in the 1980s belonged single-handedly to Gretzky; it was a decade in which he dominated the sport like no one else before or since. Playing for the Edmonton Oilers, Gretzky led his team to four Stanley Cup championships in five years. His ability to score goals and set up his teammates was unparalleled. In the 1981-82 season, Gretzky scored 92 goals, a record that still stands today.

What set Gretzky apart wasn't just his stats—it was the way he played the game. At 6 feet tall and 185 pounds, Gretzky wasn't the biggest or the fastest player on the ice, but he had an innate understanding of the game that allowed him to outthink his opponents. He could anticipate plays before they happened, finding passing lanes and creating scoring opportunities that others couldn't see. Gretzky's hockey IQ was off the charts, and he used his intelligence to dominate the game in a way that hadn't been seen before.

But it wasn't just the goals—Gretzky had an incredible ability to make everyone around him better, racking up assists and making the Oilers one of the most feared teams in hockey. Each season, his dedication to perfecting his skills and understanding of the game deepened, setting a standard for excellence and perseverance. Gretzky's training regime, often extending long after team practices had ended, showed his relentless pursuit of greatness, constantly pushing himself and his teammates to aim higher.

Perhaps one of the most defining moments of Gretzky's career came during a game against the Calgary Flames. With the game tied and only seconds left on the clock, Gretzky took the puck, weaved through multiple defenders, and scored the winning goal. But it was what he did next that truly showed his character. Instead of basking in the glory, he skated over to the rookie who had assisted the play, praising him for his effort. It was a small act, but it exemplified his leadership and humility, qualities that endeared him to fans and players alike.

But Wayne Gretzky's impact wasn't just about his on-ice performance—it was about how he changed the game of hockey forever. Before Gretzky, the NHL was known for its physical, hard-hitting style of play. Gretzky brought a new level of finesse and creativity to the game, showing that speed, skill, and intelligence could win championships. He made hockey more exciting and accessible, attracting new fans and inspiring young players around the world to pick up a stick and dream of being like "The Great One."

By the time he retired in 1999, Gretzky held 61 NHL records, including most career goals (894), assists (1,963), and points (2,857). His point total is so far ahead of anyone else in NHL history that even if you took away all of his goals, he would still be the all-time points leader based on assists alone. These records are a testament to Gretzky's dominance and ability to consistently perform at the highest level for two decades.

Wayne Gretzky's legacy is one of brilliance, innovation, and an unrelenting pursuit of excellence. He showed the world that being a champion isn't just about physical ability —it's about using your mind, your instincts, and your heart to be the best. Gretzky's story is a reminder that true greatness comes from a combination of talent, hard work, and the ability to change the game for the better.

Even today, Wayne Gretzky remains a symbol of what it means to be the best in whatever you pursue. He coined one of the most famous quotes when he said, "You miss 100% of the shots you don't take." This wasn't just advice for hockey—it was a way of life. Gretzky didn't just wait for opportunities to come to him; he created them. He took risks, made bold plays, and believed in his ability to make things happen. That mindset —always ready to take the shot and always willing to give it his all—makes him a true legend!

Scan the QR code to watch a video of Wayne Gretzky in action!

CHAPTER 50
DHYAN CHAND

THE SKILFUL MASTER

As we glide from the icy rinks where Wayne Gretzky showcased his mastery, let's shift our focus to the grassy fields where another kind of hockey legend made history long before Gretzky was even born!

Dhyan Chand, often hailed as the "Magician of Hockey," played field hockey with a finesse and skill that seemed almost supernatural. Born in Allahabad, India, Dhyan Chand's journey in field hockey began in the army, where his disciplined nature and unwavering dedication to the sport first came to light. Known for his humility and the profound respect he commanded on and off the field, Dhyan Chand was not just a player but a phenomenon that reshaped field hockey forever.

Dhyan Chand's impact on field hockey was monumental. He led India to three consecutive gold medals through the 1928, 1932, and 1936 Olympics, each victory more dominant than the last. His training regimen was as disciplined as it was rigorous, involving early morning practices and strategic game simulations that honed his incredible ball control and goal-scoring abilities. It wasn't just his skill that made him legendary, but, much like Wayne Gretzky, his ability to elevate the play of his entire team set him apart. He would often make formidable opponents seem easily manageable - and that would permeate through to the rest of his teammates. His record for most goals scored in an Olympic final still stands, a testament to his extraordinary talent and hard work.

The story of the 1936 Berlin Olympics offers a glimpse into Dhyan Chand's exceptional career. Remember how we discussed racial inequalities in Germany during the 1930s in Chapter 1? Well, much like Jesse Owens, Dhyan Chand was battling against more than just his sporting opponents that summer. During a match against Germany, with Adolf Hitler in attendance, Dhyan Chand delivered a sporting performance that was so spectacular in nature that it left the crowd, world leaders, and the opposition in awe.

Despite playing with a broken tooth and through the pain of an on-field collision, he scored an incredible three goals, securing India's third consecutive Olympic gold. This match was not just a display of Dhyan Chand's skill but also of his indomitable spirit and his leadership under pressure.

Dhyan Chand's impact went beyond his success in hockey. He strongly believed in the transformative power of sports and physical education, especially for the youth in India. By advocating for hockey and fitness, he instilled values like discipline, teamwork, and a healthy lifestyle through active participation. His focus was on nurturing young athletes and creating a healthier society.

After retiring from playing, Chand dedicated himself to mentoring and coaching the next generation of field hockey players. His work in developing training programs and coaching the national team showcased his unwavering dedication to the sport. Additionally, his efforts to promote field hockey on a global scale contributed to its enduring presence in the Olympics. His legacy is one of imagination and flair, showing that sports are not just about competition, but about expressing yourself in ways that captivate and inspire. Chand's journey teaches us that true mastery is about more than just winning—it's about leaving a lasting impression on the world with your unique talents.

CHAPTER 51
LESSONS FROM THE HEROES

WAYNE GRETZKY

ANTICIPATE THE FUTURE. DON'T JUST REACT TO WHAT'S HAPPENING—THINK AHEAD AND BE ready for what's next. Wayne's success came from his ability to see the play before it happened, teaching us that foresight and preparation are game-changers.

DHYAN CHAND

Let your passion drive you. When you love what you do, it shows in your performance and inspires others. Dhyan's magical hockey skills came from his deep love for the game, reminding us that passion is the fuel for greatness.

THE MENTALITY OF AN ATHLETE

CHAPTER 52
THE MENTALITY OF AN ATHLETE

MIND OVER MATTER

AN ATHLETE'S MENTALITY IS OFTEN UNDERAPPRECIATED WHEN IT COMES TO ANALYZING THEIR greatness. Stars like Novak Djokovic, whom we saw in Chapter 41, who are perhaps not as naturally blessed as their peers, have risen to the top of their field because their mental toughness is unrivaled. Mental training involves techniques that help you control your thoughts, sharpen your focus, and stay calm under pressure. It's like having a secret weapon that helps you perform your best when it matters most.

Whether sprinting down a track, swinging a golf club, or preparing for a big soccer match, athletes from all sports use mental training to gain an edge over their competitors. Techniques such as visualization, where you imagine executing the perfect play or race, and mindfulness, which involves being fully present in the moment, are common tools. Cognitive-behavioral strategies also play a role in helping you manage negative thoughts that can interfere with your performance. These techniques are woven into daily training, creating athletes who are not only physically but also mentally tough.

Let's dive into how some of the world's top athletes use these mental training techniques. Take, for example, a famous tennis player like Serena Williams. Before a big match, Serena uses visualization to see herself serving aces and winning points. This mental rehearsal boosts her confidence and prepares her mentally for the match ahead. Similarly, Eliud Kipchoge, the marathon runner who broke the two-hour barrier for the marathon, uses mindfulness to maintain focus during his long, grueling races. He concentrates on his breathing and stride, staying in the moment to ward off any mental fatigue that might slow him down.

These techniques are not just for individual athletes. Teams can use them, too. For instance, before a big game, a soccer team might engage in a group visualization session, where they picture themselves executing perfect plays and winning the game. This not only prepares them mentally but also builds team cohesion and spirit.

Loads of research back the benefits of mental training. For starters, athletes who engage in mental training often show improved concentration. They can better focus during competitions, tuning out distractions like a noisy crowd or bad weather. Stress management is another significant benefit. Sports can be stressful, and being able to manage that stress is crucial. Athletes trained in mindfulness and relaxation techniques can keep their cool under pressure, performing at their best when it counts.

Mental training enhances the ability to perform under pressure. It prepares athletes for the stress of competition, so when they face a crucial point in a game or match, they're more likely to succeed. It's like they've been there a hundred times before, even if it's just in their minds.

So, how can you start implementing these mental training techniques into your routine? It's simpler than you might think. Start small with something like basic breathing exercises to help calm your nerves before a game. Practice visualizing successful plays or races for a few minutes each day. Over time, these mental exercises will become a natural part of your training.

Coaches and sports psychologists are crucial in developing effective mental training programs. They can help tailor these techniques to fit the specific needs of different sports and individual athletes, ensuring the mental training is as effective as possible. Whether through one-on-one sessions or team workshops, the right guidance can make a huge difference in how well these techniques are adopted and how effective they are in helping athletes reach their full potential.

By incorporating mental training into their overall practice routines, athletes can develop a strong mental edge that complements their physical skills, setting them up for success in every competition they face.

Imagine you're at the start line, your heart pounding as you gaze down the track. It's the final race, and everyone's eyes are on you. The weight of expectations can feel heavier than the world on your shoulders. This weight is performance pressure, and it comes from everywhere: your own desire to win, your coach's advice, your family's hopes, and the cheers or silence of the crowd watching. This pressure can push you to achieve great things, but it can also be overwhelming, causing nerves that might trip you up when you least want them to.

Understanding where this pressure comes from is the first step in handling it. It's not just about the expectations others have for you but also the standards you set for yourself. You might feel compelled to win to make your family proud or to live up to your coach's rigorous training. Fans might expect spectacular results based on your past performances. All these can heighten the sense of urgency and tension during competitions. While this can motivate you to perform well, it can also lead to anxiety and fear of failure, affecting your performance negatively.

Now, let's talk about some real strategies to tackle this pressure head-on. First off, setting realistic goals is crucial. It's great to aim high, but unreachable goals can make you feel like you're falling short, increasing pressure and disappointment. Break your goals into smaller, manageable targets that you can hit step by step. This way, each success builds your confidence.

Focusing on the process rather than just the outcome can also significantly reduce pressure. Instead of obsessing over winning, concentrate on performing your best. Think about the technique your coach has been drilling into you or the strategy you've been perfecting during practice. This shift in focus helps you stay in the moment and reduces the anxiety about what the final scoreboard will say.

Pre-performance routines are another key strategy. These are consistent habits or activities you do before a game or race that help settle your nerves. It could be listening to a specific song, a warm-up routine, or a series of stretches. These routines signal to your body and mind that it's time to perform, providing a sense of familiarity and comfort and bringing a sense of control amidst the chaos of competition.

Let's look at some real-life heroes to bring these ideas to life. Consider a golfer on the 18th hole with one shot to win the tournament. The golfer who succeeds is the one who can set aside the crowd's roars and focus solely on the shot, just as they've practiced countless times. Or think about a swimmer in the Olympics, where a fraction of a second can mean the difference between a medal and nothing. The swimmers who break records are the ones who use techniques like visualization to see themselves touching the wall first, feeling the water glide past them perfectly as they swim.

Lastly, dealing with performance pressure is not a one-off task. It requires building a solid support system of family, friends, coaches, and possibly sports psychologists who understand and help manage the pressures you face. Regularly practicing mental resilience skills, like positive self-talk and mindfulness, strengthens your ability to handle stress. Learning from past performances, both good and bad, also prepares you for future challenges.

Remember, the key is to recognize the signs of pressure and to use these strategies actively to keep your cool, turning what could be a barrier into a stepping stone to greatness. As you continue to grow in your sport, these experiences with pressure will equip you to handle bigger stages and tougher competitions, enhancing your performance and your love for the game.

As we wrap up this chapter, keep in mind that overcoming performance pressure isn't just about handling the stress of the big moments—it's about transforming these moments into opportunities for growth and excellence. Moving forward, the skills you develop here will help you not only in sports but in every challenge you face in life, teaching you resilience, focus, and the real meaning of victory.

FULL TIME!

CHAPTER 53
BONUS CHAPTERS!

CANT' GET ENOUGH SPORT?!

Scan the secret QR code hidden in the book to unlock exciting **bonus chapters** packed with jaw-dropping sports stories!

Discover the longest matches ever played, where athletes battled for hours in the ultimate test of endurance. Plus, meet young sporting prodigies who amazed the world with their incredible talents at an early age.

Don't miss out—these hidden chapters are waiting just for you!

CHAPTER 54
FULL TIME!

As we reach the final whistle of our journey through "The Most Inspiring Sports Stories of All Time for Kids!" it's time to reflect on the incredible athletes and teams whose stories we've shared. From the perseverance of Jesse Owens and Wilma Rudolph to the mastery and activism of Muhammad Ali, and from the sheer courage of Terry Fox and Bethany Hamilton to the unexpected triumphs of the 1980 US Hockey team and Leicester City FC, we've seen a common thread—determination and resilience.

These athletes came from different backgrounds, faced unique challenges, and achieved remarkable feats. Remember how Muhammad Ali stood up for his beliefs or how Terry Fox ran across Canada to raise awareness for cancer research despite his own battle with the disease? These stories aren't just about sports; they're lessons in overcoming adversity, achieving dreams through hard work, and the importance of sportsmanship and integrity.

Sports are more than just games. They are a powerful platform for cultural expression, social change, and global unity. Athletes like these have broken down barriers and used their platforms to promote equality and community well-being. They show us that being an athlete also involves contributing to society and improving the world.

We also learned about the advancements in sports science, nutrition, and mental training that help athletes perform at their best. These tools are not just for the elite; they are lessons for all of us about taking care of our bodies and minds.

Many athletes we discussed have successfully transitioned from competition to other roles in business, philanthropy, and mentorship, proving that the skills and values learned in sports—like leadership, teamwork, and perseverance—are invaluable in all areas of life.

Now, it's your turn. Whether you play sports just for fun or dream of becoming a professional athlete, remember the values of dedication, teamwork, and perseverance. See challenges as opportunities to grow, and always strive to do your best. Engage in sports at any level. It's not just about winning games but also about enjoying the game, staying healthy, and learning important life lessons.

So, lace up your sneakers, grab your gear, and step onto the field or court. Participate, support your peers, and be an active member of your sports community. And remember, no matter where you are or what sport you play, you have the power to make a difference—just like the athletes we've read about.

Sports have the incredible power to inspire us, shape our societies, and bridge cultural divides. As you close this book, I hope you feel renewed hope and motivation to pursue your passions in sports and beyond. Remember, every game played, every race run and every shot taken can be a step toward building a better world.

Let's keep playing, keep dreaming, and keep pushing our limits. The game is never really over; it's just the beginning of your next great adventure.

WOULD YOU LIKE YOUR NEXT BOOK FOR FREE?

Your feedback on "The Most Inspiring Sports Stories of All Time for Kids!" Is **incredibly valuable to me**. If you enjoyed the book, I would greatly appreciate your thoughts.

As an author, reviews are not just a form of feedback, **they are the cornerstone of my career**. Your review can make a significant difference.

I'm so committed to this belief that I'd like to **offer you a free copy** of any of the 30+ books I've written. The most popular ones include illustrated biographies of Jude Bellingham, Lionel Messi, and Cristiano Ronaldo. (Ages 6-9)

Or, for slightly older audiences, I've got The Most Inspirational Women's Soccer Stories of All Time - or the classic bestseller The Most Amazing Soccer Stories of All Time!

Email me at mikelangdon1@gmail.com with the Subject line: FREE BOOK.

I'll personally respond to your email to arrange the best shipping address for your book.

Michael Langdon

Instagram: @itsmikelangdon

TRIVIA TIME!

QUESTIONS

1. WHERE DID JESSE OWENS WIN FOUR GOLD MEDALS?
   - A) 1948 London Olympics
   - B) 1936 Berlin Olympics
   - C) 1960 Rome Olympics
   - D) 1924 Paris Olympics

2. What health challenges did Wilma Rudolph face in her early years?
   - A) Chickenpox and measles
   - B) Asthma and diabetes
   - C) Double pneumonia, scarlet fever, and polio
   - D) Tuberculosis and mumps

3. What was the name of Terry Fox's run to raise awareness and funds for cancer research?
   - A) Run for Life
   - B) Hope Marathon
   - C) Marathon of Hope
   - D) Cancer Run

. . .

4. How far did Terry Fox run during his Marathon of Hope before he had to stop?
   - A) 3,000 kilometers
   - B) 4,500 kilometers
   - C) 5,300 kilometers
   - D) 6,200 kilometers

5. Who is known for the quote, "I ain't got no quarrel with them Viet Cong"?
   - A) Jesse Owens
   - B) Muhammad Ali
   - C) Terry Fox
   - D) Wilma Rudolph

6. What nickname was given to Muhammad Ali for his bold predictions and poetic speeches?
   - A) The Fighter
   - B) The Legend
   - C) The Champion
   - D) The Greatest

7. Which significant bout highlighted the legacy of two famous boxing families, featuring Laila Ali?
   - A) Ali/Tyson
   - B) Ali/Holmes
   - C) Ali/Frazier IV
   - D) Ali/Foreman

8. What was the main focus of Laila Ali's advocacy beyond her boxing career?
   - A) Environmental issues
   - B) Women's rights and empowerment
   - C) Economic development
   - D) Technological innovation

9. What distinctive feature is Bradley Wiggins known for?
   - A) His colorful helmet
   - B) His sideburns

- C) His cycling shoes
- D) His sunglasses

10. In which year did Bradley Wiggins become the first British cyclist to win the Tour de France?
- A) 2008
- B) 2010
- C) 2012
- D) 2014

11. How many World Championships did Michael Schumacher win in his Formula 1 career?
- A) Five
- B) Six
- C) Seven
- D) Eight

12. What charitable cause did Michael Schumacher advocate for beyond his racing career?
- A) Environmental conservation
- B) Road safety
- C) Animal rights
- D) Educational reform

13. How old was Bethany Hamilton when she was attacked by a shark?
- A) 10
- B) 13
- C) 15
- D) 17

14. What technique did Michael Phelps revolutionize in swimming?
- A) Butterfly stroke
- B) Freestyle stroke
- C) Underwater dolphin kick
- D) Backstroke start

. . .

15. Which team did Jim Abbott pitch a no-hitter for?
   - A) California Angels
   - B) New York Yankees
   - C) Chicago White Sox
   - D) Milwaukee Brewers

16. Who helped Derek Redmond finish his 400m race at the 1992 Barcelona Olympics?
   - A) His coach
   - B) His teammate
   - C) His father
   - D) A fellow competitor

17. What was the nickname given to the 1980 US Hockey Team's victory over the Soviet Union?
   - A) Miracle on Ice
   - B) Ice Champions
   - C) Winter Victory
   - D) Cold War Clash

18. Who was the head coach of the 1980 US Hockey Team?
   - A) Herb Brooks
   - B) Scotty Bowman
   - C) Mike Eruzione
   - D) Al Michaels

19. What were the odds of Leicester City winning the Premier League at the beginning of the 2015-2016 season?
   - A) 1000-1
   - B) 5000-1
   - C) 2000-1
   - D) 100-1

. . .

20. Which player scored in 11 consecutive Premier League matches for Leicester City during their 2015-2016 season?
- A) Riyad Mahrez
- B) Jamie Vardy
- C) N'Golo Kanté
- D) Wes Morgan

21. At which Olympic Games did Nadia Comăneci score the first perfect 10 in gymnastics?
- A) 1972 Munich Olympics
- B) 1976 Montreal Olympics
- C) 1980 Moscow Olympics
- D) 1984 Los Angeles Olympics

22. How old was Nadia Comăneci when she achieved her perfect 10?
- A) 12
- B) 14
- C) 16
- D) 18

23. What is the notable diving achievement of Greg Louganis at the 1982 World Championships?
- A) Winning gold in three events
- B) Performing the highest difficulty dive
- C) Receiving perfect 10 scores from all seven judges
- D) Setting a new world record for highest dive

24. What unique scoring achievement did Annika Sörenstam accomplish at the Standard Register PING tournament in 2001?
- A) Scoring a perfect round of 18
- B) Shooting a score of 59
- C) Winning by 15 strokes
- D) Making 10 consecutive birdies

25. From which city in Argentina does Lionel Messi originate?

- A) Buenos Aires
- B) Rosario
- C) Córdoba
- D) Mendoza

26. Which football club's academy did Lionel Messi join at the age of 13?
    - A) Real Madrid
    - B) Manchester United
    - C) FC Barcelona
    - D) Paris Saint-Germain

27. What major health challenge did Lionel Messi overcome in his youth?
    - A) Diabetes
    - B) Growth hormone deficiency
    - C) Asthma
    - D) Heart condition

28. How many Super Bowl titles has Tom Brady won?
    - A) 5
    - B) 6
    - C) 7
    - D) 8

29. What was Babe Ruth's nickname?
    - A) The Home Run King
    - B) The Sultan of Swat
    - C) The Big Bambino
    - D) The Baseball God

30. For which team did Babe Ruth start his career as a pitcher?
    - A) New York Yankees
    - B) Boston Red Sox
    - C) Chicago Cubs
    - D) St. Louis Cardinals

. . .

31. Which young fan did Babe Ruth promise to hit a home run for in the 1926 World Series?
   - A) Tommy Jones
   - B) Johnny Sylvester
   - C) Billy Madison
   - D) Jimmy Carter

32. How many World Series titles did Babe Ruth win with the New York Yankees?
   - A) 5
   - B) 6
   - C) 7
   - D) 8

33. What was Larry Bird known for that also made him a psychological strategist against his opponents?
   - A) His height
   - B) His trash-talking
   - C) His physical strength
   - D) His running speed

34. During which NBA Finals game did Larry Bird play despite the sweltering heat due to a failed air conditioning system, showcasing his mental and physical toughness?
   - A) 1984 NBA Finals, Game 5
   - B) 1986 NBA Finals, Game 3
   - C) 1987 NBA Finals, Game 4
   - D) 1985 NBA Finals, Game 6

35. What is Kareem Abdul-Jabbar's signature move?
   - A) The Dunk
   - B) The Layup
   - C) The Skyhook
   - D) The Fadeaway

36. Which 1980 NBA Finals game did Kareem Abdul-Jabbar score 40 points despite an ankle injury?

- A) Game 1
- B) Game 3
- C) Game 5
- D) Game 6

37. How many Grand Slam titles has Roger Federer won?
  - A) 18
  - B) 19
  - C) 20
  - D) 21

38. What was the epic match that Roger Federer played against Rafael Nadal, often called the greatest in tennis history?
  - A) 2007 Wimbledon final
  - B) 2008 Wimbledon final
  - C) 2009 Wimbledon final
  - D) 2010 Wimbledon final

39. What nickname is Novak Djokovic known by, reflecting his resilience and stamina on the court?
  - A) The Joker
  - B) The Iron Man of Tennis
  - C) The King of Clay
  - D) The Tennis Titan

40. As of August 2024, how many Grand Slam titles has Novak Djokovic won?
  - A) 21
  - B) 22
  - C) 23
  - D) 24

ANSWERS

1. B) 1936 Berlin Olympics
2. C) Double pneumonia, scarlet fever, and polio
3. C) Marathon of Hope

4. C) 5,300 kilometers

5. B) Muhammad Ali

6. D) The Greatest

7. C) Ali/Frazier IV

8. B) Women's rights and empowerment

9. B) His sideburns

10. C) 2012

11. C) Seven

12. B) Road safety

13. B) 13

14. C) Underwater dolphin kick

15. B) New York Yankees

16. C) His father

17. A) Miracle on Ice

18. A) Herb Brooks

19. B) 5000-1

20. B) Jamie Vardy

21. B) 1976 Montreal Olympics

22. B) 14

23. C) Receiving perfect 10 scores from all seven judges

24. B) Shooting a score of 59

25. B) Rosario

26. C) FC Barcelona

27. B) Growth hormone deficiency

28. C) 7

29. B) The Sultan of Swat

30. B) Boston Red Sox

31. B) Johnny Sylvester

32. C) 7

33. B) His trash-talking

34. A) 1984 NBA Finals, Game 5

35. C) The Skyhook

36. C) Game 5

37. C) 20

38. B) 2008 Wimbledon final

39. B) The Iron Man of Tennis

40. D) 24